forever
LOVE

CELESTE O. NORFLEET

forever LOVE

HARLEQUIN®

entertain, enrich, inspire™

Recycling programs
for this product may
not exist in your area.

FOREVER LOVE

ISBN-13: 978-0-373-53490-6

Copyright © 2012 by Celeste O. Norfleet

Dear Reader,

As always, thank you for your support and dedication
to the Mamma Lou Matchmaker series. It's a pleasure
to bring you another novel featuring the indomitable
octogenarian Louise "Mamma Lou" Gates. *Forever Love*
is very special to me because it brings together Louise
and her sister Emma's family. These two great families—
the Gates clan of Crescent Island and the Washingtons
of Philadelphia—share Mamma Lou as their surrogate
matriarch. In *Forever Love* you will meet Gia Duncan
and be reintroduced to Keith Washington, a character I
originally introduced several years ago in a novel entitled
Only You. It has always been my intent to join these two
wonderful families, and I'm delighted to now bring you
Forever Love.

Watch for more Mamma Lou Matchmaker series novels
coming soon, including the event we've all been waiting
for, Louise and Otis's wedding—*In the Name of Love!*

Celeste O. Norfleet

www.celesteonorfleet.wordpress.com

Mamma Lou Matchmaker Series Family Tree

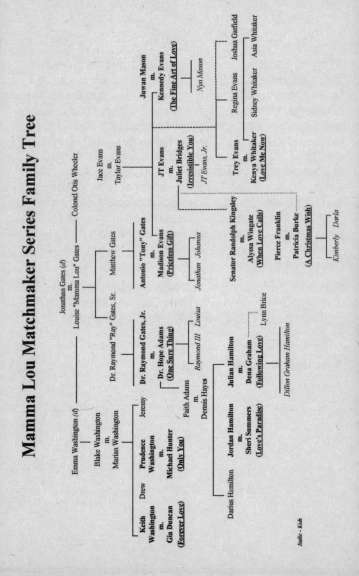

Italic - Kids

To Fate & Fortune

Prologue

It was barely after dawn when Keith Washington parked his car on the upper level and walked across the connecting bridge to the Washington & Associates Law Firm office building. He pressed the elevator button to the top floor, unlocked the outer doors and strolled inside. As soon as he went to turn off the alarm, he paused. It was already off. He'd been the last person out of the office late last night and he knew he had turned off the lights and activated the alarm system. He looked around, knowing there was only one explanation: somebody was already there.

Few people had the key to get in and even fewer had the code to disable the alarm. He looked around. Nothing seemed disturbed in the lobby or reception area. He looked up at the glass-covered atrium ceiling. The dimly muted lighting revealed nothing. Still, he knew he wasn't alone.

Keith walked around the reception desk and continued down the main hallway to the executive suites. As he approached his office he saw a thin shaft of light coming from the conference room at the far end of the hall. He continued walking. As he approached he heard low voices in conversation.

He pushed the cracked door open to see his two brothers already seated at the conference table. Drew and Jeremy looked up as soon as he entered. "I guess you've heard we have a serious situation," Keith said.

"That's an understatement," Drew corrected.

Jeremy nodded soberly. "So, what are we gonna do?"

Keith walked over and picked up the last cup of coffee left in the takeout holder on the table. He took a sip and leaned his elbows on the back of the chair across from his brothers. "Okay, we all knew this was gonna come at us one day."

"Yeah, one day, but not now, I don't have time for this," Drew said. "Now that Dad's running for reelection, my caseload has doubled with more clients coming in every week."

"None of us have the time," Keith said, "but the situation's here and we have to deal with it."

"You're the two oldest," Jeremy reminded them in warning.

"You know that doesn't mean anything," Drew said.

"What we need to do is set a plan in motion. Any suggestions?"

"Yeah, run like hell," Jeremy joked. Drew and Keith smiled.

"That would be nice, but I don't think it's gonna solve the main problem. We have a couple of weeks at best before…"

Drew looked up quickly. "A couple of weeks," he repeated.

Keith nodded. "That's what I'm hearing, although it may be less. Mom said she might be here for the Prudence and Speed's children's benefit ball. So she may come sooner."

"That's next Saturday—just over a week," Jeremy said, shaking his head, already forlorn by the inevitable. "You know there's no way we're getting out of this."

"No, we'll be fine. We just have to focus and come up with a viable plan," Keith said calmly. As lead attorney for the law firm, he'd faced all types of challenges. He never gave up and never backed down from a fight. But this was different. This could change his perfectly ordered life forever, and that he couldn't have.

Drew laughed. "A plan, are you kidding? There's no way we can win this one. She's too good."

"I vote we just leave town," Jeremy said.

"All of us—at the same time—with an election coming— a bit obvious, don't you think?" Keith said. "You know, maybe we're just overestimating this. Maybe it's not as bad as we think."

"Yes, it is," both Drew and Jeremy said in unison. They all chuckled.

"Okay, bottom line, someone's gonna have to keep her distracted. She can't get to all of us at one time."

"I say the oldest takes the bullet," Jeremy suggested.

"I second that," Drew added without skipping a beat.

They turned to Keith. He laughed heartily, then instantly stopped. "Not funny. We're all in this together. If one of us goes down, we all go down. It's only a matter of time after that. I say we stick together—a united front. That's the only way to get out of this unscathed. That's where our cousins, Tony and Raymond, Mamma Lou's first two victims, went wrong, they didn't stick together." He looked from face to face. Each brother slowly nodded his agreement. Keith nodded, as well. "Okay, good."

They all knew the solution was obvious. One of them would have to step up and block the others. Keith stood and walked over to a stained-glass wall cabinet at the back of the room. Drew and Jeremy watched. He opened it and pulled out a pearl and onyx case. He brought it over to the table and set it down. He opened it and took out one cigar.

He rolled it between his fingers, then held it beneath his nose and inhaled deeply. Nodding his approval, he looked at his brothers and then, using the cutters, clipped it in half. Three heads nodded. They understood.

Keith pulled the rest of the cigars out of the humidifier and placed two back in along with the half cigar. He shook it around gently and then set the case back on the table facing away from them. Jeremy and Drew reached in and pulled out a cigar. There was only one left. Without even choosing, it was instantly obvious who'd lost.

Chapter 1

Standing in the back of a town hall meeting, Gia Duncan looked at her watch again. She was itching to get this thing started. This was her opening act and it could make or break her and her organization's future. This was a monumental undertaking—one that had never been openly tried. Each time the main door opened, she held her breath and looked over anxiously, hoping this was it. Her edginess was just about to get the better of her. "Come on, come on," she muttered under her breath.

"What did you say?" Bill asked, leaning over to her.

"Nothing, just talking to myself," she said quietly, briefly glancing over to her business associate, Bill Axelby.

"Gia, you have to calm down," Bill whispered again.

"You know this is ridiculous. He's an hour and a half late. Seriously, who does he think he is? Is the whole world just supposed to stop and wait for him to decide when he's gonna get here?"

"He's not scheduled to be here until four. Besides, he's the last speaker to go on. And by the looks of that guy up there now, we're gonna be here for the rest of the night."

"That's not the point," she said, staring at the empty chair on the stage. It was obvious that her anxiousness was getting harder and harder to mask.

"Gia, everything will go as planned, trust me. We went over this a dozen times. Everybody knows what they need to do."

She nodded. "Yeah, I hope so."

"Never get discouraged when you're doing the right thing."

She nodded. Bill was right. He repeated her grandmother's words exactly. Her grandmother would have never been as anxious as she was now. And even if she was, you'd never see it. Julia Duncan was the ultimate fighter. She had courage, integrity and intelligence—a lethal combination that scared politicians to the core. But most of all, she was always in control.

She had never gone up against someone like this though she had had the opportunity plenty of times. It seemed her grandmother, like most of the city of Philadelphia, believed Blake Washington and his family were superstars. They could do no wrong. And the popularity index tipping over seventy-eight percent proved it.

The main door opened again. She turned to look. It wasn't him. "Crap," she muttered.

Bill opened the program he'd received earlier. "Who is this guy and what's he running for again?"

"His name is Preston Hodge and he's running for city council. He's thirty-one years old, single, a stockbroker and he wants Lester Jameson's council seat since he's running against Blake Washington for mayor," their assistant, Bonnie Axelby informed them. "He's good and has some really forward-thinking ideas. I think he's really going places in this city."

Both Gia and Bill turned to her. She smiled happily. "What?" she said, surprised to see their stunned faces. "I do my research. I know the personal and professional background of just about everybody on the ballot."

Gia shook her head. "Bonnie, I'm impressed."

"Thanks."

"Come on, Bill, this is totally interesting," Bonnie, Bill's younger sister, said excitedly. "Just think about it, this is what our Founding Fathers meant when they created the democratic process. Every man has an equal opportunity to get up and expand on the issues and toss his hat into the political ring."

Gia looked at their young assistant. Her naïveté was admirable, but Gia knew it would soon vanish just like the belief in Santa Claus and the Easter Bunny. Sadly, innocence lost can never be regained.

She remembered her own moments of true realization.

She was idealistic and innocently full of hope and ambition. She once believed that right would always triumph and that good always won over bad, but that was a long time ago. Gullible was what her grandfather had called her the day he kicked her out. That day her father and grandfather had taught her the ways of their world. It was a basic philosophy that they lived their lives by: only money matters.

But she soon learned that money and power weren't the answer, and she intended to prove it. They expected her to fail and come running back to them, but she had proved them wrong.

She was never going to let another rich man take advantage of her. Her paternal grandfather controlled her grandmother, and her father usurped her mother. When she refused to take it anymore he divorced her. There was no way she was going to follow their mistakes, not even for love. She was too strong for that. Her last two ex-boyfriends found that out quickly.

She knew better. Politics was a dirty business that thrived on the money and power and only those with deep pockets and unlimited resources made it to the top. She'd learned quickly that it wasn't about the politics of governing and doing the right thing; it was about the prestige and power of ultimate control.

She looked around at the crowded assembly. No one was really paying much attention to the current speaker. Partly because everyone had heard his type of rhetoric a dozen times before and partly because he was just plain boring. It was obvious everyone was waiting for the same person to arrive—the mayor. Coincidentally, just then, Preston Hodge mentioned the mayor's endorsement and the crowd applauded and cheered.

She shook her head. They were like lemmings jumping off a cliff. Just mention his name and the crowd cheers. Granted, as politicians go, he wasn't the worst, but she just assumed he hadn't been found out yet. Yes, there were others with much worse reputations. But they weren't the current mayor of Philadelphia and they weren't running for a second term, having failed miserably to get much of anything done in the first.

This wasn't personal, and political affiliation had nothing to do with this. She was an independent, meaning she voted for the best candidate. She was well informed and wanted other voters to be just as prepared for whom they were casting their vote. Four years was a long time to sit and do nothing while the city crumbled apart beneath their feet.

"Oh, my God, there he is, there he is," Bonnie said excitedly.

Gia looked over at the main door quickly. Wouldn't you know it, the second she wasn't paying attention, he arrived, but she didn't see him. "The mayor, where is he? I don't see him."

"No, not the mayor, his oldest son, Keith Washington. He's over there," she said dreamily, letting her voice trail softly as she stared with her eyes glazed over. "Damn," she said, exhaling at length, her voice raised two octaves. "He's even more gorgeous in person than in his pictures on the internet. No wonder he's got half the women in the city knocking down his door. Look at him, he's just too, too sexy, isn't he?"

"Bonnie, focus. You sound like a groupie," Bill snapped tightly through gritted teeth. She rolled her eyes at her brother's impatience with her. As half brother and half sister, theirs wasn't an easy alliance. "You do this all the time," he continued. "You never take anything seriously. This is a job. It's important. Not everyone is sitting on a massive trust fund like you. We don't have—"

"Hey, it's not my fault you gambled and blew through all your money in a day and a half," Bonnie said, interrupting his tirade. "Just because you're broke…"

"I'm not broke," Bill snapped again. "I have money. I invest. My money's tied up in my future."

"Okay. Okay, enough," Gia whispered, seeing that their conversation was beginning to draw attention. "Where is he, Bonnie?" she asked, looking at the main entrance again.

"There he is, over by the side door," Bonnie said, completely ignoring her brother. "Isn't he gorgeous?" she said rhetorically. Gia didn't respond and Bill just shook his head.

"Okay, can we get back to reality now? If Keith Washington is here, that means the mayor is here, too. Get ready."

Gia nodded with excitement and then glanced

at the side door again. "So that's Keith Washington." Good Lord, Bonnie was right. Just looking at him made her stomach flutter excitedly. The photos she'd seen didn't come close to what he looked like in person.

She knew who he was, of course; most Philadelphians did. But like everyone involved in the mayoral race, she had also researched him online, getting about what she had expected. According to his business profile, he was the typical big-city attorney working in a typical big-city law office. He specialized in political lawsuits, working mostly in New York, Washington, D.C., and Philadelphia.

There was nothing in his résumé and profile that was out of the ordinary. And that in and of itself made her suspicious. She knew a PR job when she saw one. It was obvious that the Washington family publicity machine had whitewashed everything that appeared in their online profiles. It was something her grandfather and father did, as well. She wondered what he was really like. Driven, calculating and arrogant, she quickly assessed.

His mother was a judge, his father was mayor, his two brothers were attorneys and his sister was a fashion merchandiser and also married to the number-one quarterback on the Philadelphia Knights football team. Bottom line, Keith had a family with power, prestige and clout. But she knew there was more to him than what she had read in his pristine online bio and what she saw of him standing across the room.

He was tall, over six feet, and standing majestic

with broad shoulders and long, slightly bowed muscular legs. He wore an expensive suit that looked as if it had been tailored onto his body, and beneath, she could only imagine the fine firmness of his lean muscled body. No lie, the man was seriously built and the ease with which he carried himself showed that he was very sure of himself. Control and confidence covered him like a lover's embrace.

She saw his face as he looked around the hall. He was classically handsome with a firm angular jaw and warm brown bedroom eyes. He had full sensual lips that looked tender and succulent. Gia smiled to herself as several "I wonder…" stray thoughts eased into her mind. Her mouth moistened and her legs tightened as the itch of wondering grew stronger.

"Aren't you supposed to be seated up front?" Bill asked.

Gia startled, ending her erotic musings as Bonnie sucked her teeth and shook her head. "Seriously, who has a town hall meeting on a Monday evening?"

"Bonnie," Bill snarled.

"Fine, I'm going." Then she looked at Gia and smiled. "I'm right, aren't I? He's too, too sexy."

Gia didn't respond. She couldn't. Her mouth had gone bone dry.

Chapter 2

It had been a long day and now Keith Washington sat in the backseat of his father's SUV looking over the event's program. It was a typical small-venue town hall meeting. It was time-consuming and off the usual grid, but no big deal. Though this wasn't one he'd sanctioned.

There were several sponsors involved, some of whom he didn't know. That, he didn't like. But this was a favor set up by his father for an old friend who'd been working at the community center for years. Having Blake show up brought people out, and that helped the event and the center. But ultimately he'd wished he had more information up front about the other sponsors. He knew in a setting like this, anything could happen.

The last-minute strategy meeting in the backseat of his father's SUV came to an end just as the car stopped. Keith sent a text to his assistant, who was already inside; there were no last-second changes. Everything was as planned. They were ready and everything was set. It was time. "Are you ready for this?" he asked his father before getting out.

Blake smiled and nodded. "I am. These are my constituents, but they aren't just the people voting for me. These are the people hoping and praying that I make their lives better. I know it's small compara- tively, but the second I become complacent about the small things is the time I need to get out of office."

Keith nodded. He knew his father was right. Each and every campaign appearance was essential, not only for the candidate, but also for the office. He knew his father would give one hundred percent and more. "That's exactly the answer we need. Let's do this."

Just as Keith got out of the SUV, Blake's cell phone rang. "It's your mother. Go ahead in, I'm right behind you," Blake said, answering the cell phone smiling.

Keith nodded and continued walking inside. Megan Keats, the law firm's publicist and the cam- paign's PR specialist, met him at the door and handed him a few notes. He read them quickly, then shook hands and briefly spoke with a few associates and businessmen as he entered. The news media were there. He smiled, answered a few questions, then excused himself and headed to the main hall. He stopped at the side entrance and looked back. His father had entered the building and was smiling, shaking hands and chatting briefly with those standing around waiting. He took a few photos, waved and shook more hands.

Keith shook his head. Practicing legislative and regulatory law was nothing compared to being his father's political strategist and campaign manager. In that position he headed an impressive inner circle of senior advisers that included a media strategist, a communications and policy research director, a chief pollster and a financial director. And every day dozens of résumés were delivered for his vetting.

Everyone wanted to get on board the campaign train because everyone knew this was only the beginning. His father's political aspirations were modest, but the party was already looking a decade ahead to a very prominent Washington, D.C., position.

Keith stepped inside the main hall and looked around. The small area was packed as he had expected. His father always drew a crowd. Preston Hodge was at the podium speaking. Keith watched him for a few seconds. He'd already assessed Preston as a nonthreat. Still, he was a wild card. He had bold aspirations and a heart to do well, but his troubled background would either hold him back or propel him forward.

The next person he saw on stage was Lester Jameson, his father's political opponent. He knew he'd already spoken. Keith smiled. What Lester didn't know was that was exactly as he'd planned it, leaving his father to go last. Lester was a smug, condescending man whose deep pockets matched his father's but whose political need for power was far too grandiose. Plus, he carried enough baggage to sink the *Titanic* all over again. He was desperate and he was treacherous—two very dangerous attributes.

"All set," Blake said, placing his hand on Keith's shoulder.

"Yeah, in a few minutes," Keith said, still looking around. He took a deep uneasy breath and released it slowly, shaking his head. "This doesn't feel right, Dad," he said, nodding at the men standing just inside the entranceway. "You know you really don't have to do this. All the polls confirm it. You're eight points ahead."

"With five points give or take. This election is still too close to call. Jameson still has a very strong following. It could still go either way."

"But you don't really need this exposure."

"And that's exactly why I'm doing this, Keith. It's not about the polls or the numbers or the exposure. It's about pressing flesh, shaking hands and getting to know my constituents. It's about getting out of the office and meeting the people who matter. You know I've always done this and I'm gonna continue to do it even after I'm out of office."

Keith nodded. He knew his father was right. Blake Washington loved being with people, and people loved being with him.

Preston finished to a very impressive round of applause. Blake's friend Ace Miller stood up to the podium and, seeing Keith, nodded. Keith opened the door as the announcement was made. Blake entered and everyone turned to see him walk in smiling and waving. He shook hands all the way to the podium. Keith stood, watching Lester. The jealous fire in his eyes was obvious.

Moments later Blake stepped up to the podium and shook hands with his friend and the other candidates on the stage. He took the microphone as the open show of praise intensified. He nodded his head gratefully as the crowd began to settle down. He thanked everybody for coming, then walked down into the crowd and spoke briefly about his hopes and plans for the future of the city. Applause and standing ovations praised the speech throughout. Afterward he took questions and listened to comments and concerns. That's when everything changed.

A few very positive comments and insightful questions began the segment. Then a young man stood at the center microphone. But to everyone's stunned surprise, his comment wasn't just a simple concern of interest about the general welfare of the city. It was accusatory and aggressive, laced with specific unverified allegations about corruption and misappropriations of funds.

The next few comments continued on the same vein of polite, but assertive aggression. Several people in the audience grumbled in defense of the mayor as it became obvious that this was an ambush. These weren't constituents here to speak and air their concerns with their mayor. These were professional rabble-rousers put in place to stir trouble.

Keith knew a setup when he saw one, but that didn't concern him. He knew his father would handle the situation easily. What concerned him was that this was a strategically formulated plan and he knew someone sitting in this very room was responsible. The people asking questions were merely mouthpiece puppets—somebody worked the strings.

He looked around the room with more intent. Everyone was looking at his father, paying attention to what was going on, except for a man across the hall looking directly at him. The smug gleeful expression on his face was evident. This was the puppeteer he was looking for.

Keith didn't recognize him at first, and then he did. He'd seen him a few times. He worked for a community service organization, and right now that satisfied smirk on his face was a dead giveaway.

Keith watched as he leaned over and said something to the woman standing beside him. She turned and looked across the room. Their eyes met and held. Keith's expression didn't change, nor did hers. After a few seconds she looked away quickly, but her companion continued to stare in an almost rapturous delight. He wasn't just happy, he was elated. This was definitely personal. Then it apparently occurred to him that his expression betrayed more than he intended and he quickly turned away. He spoke to the woman beside him again, and then seconds later he walked off in the opposite direction.

Keith watched him cut through the crowd and head to the exit on the other side of the hall. When he got to the door, he turned for one last smirk, then walked out.

Keith refocused on his father. Blake had been answering questions and concerns with his usual calm and even-tempered consideration. He stayed focused and regained his momentum quickly. It was only obvious to the few who knew him well that he'd been caught off guard at first. Like Keith, his father was a master at suppressing emotions through years of courtroom confrontations. He glanced at Keith in a brief instance. Keith nodded his understanding. Blake was back in full control, although the swell of emotions around him had escalated. Tensions were rising and only Blake's calm, assertive answers seemed to quell the inevitable aggressions. Keith turned back to the woman still standing across the hall. She seemed engrossed in what was going on around her. Her expression was placid, radiating the slightest trace of inner pride that was more mischievous than menacing. He knew she was part of this, as well. But unlike her associate, she looked surprisingly impressed with his father.

Keith walked over slowly, assessing her physical attributes, while her attention stayed focused on his father. She was certainly attractive in her tailored business suite and high heels. He eagerly admired her long shapely legs and her taut rear. Both sent a lustful image of horizontal pleasure through his mind. She had dark hair that brushed her shoulders and flowed easily each time she turned her head. And beyond that, her soft honey-toned complexion, high cheekbones and full luscious lips tinted with a soft blush of color gave him a few less than gentlemanly ideas.

He stood behind her and watched as she focused on the questions and comments. Then all of a sudden she looked around, scanning the area purposefully. Because of the mayor's presence and the onslaught of negative campaign rhetoric, it had gotten even more crowded than before. Keith watched, knowing she was looking for him. He smiled, enjoying her hunt. All of a sudden the cat was looking for the mouse—*interesting*. He licked his lips and leaned down close to her ear. "I'm here, behind you," he whispered softly.

Gia inhaled a spicy heavenly aroma. She whipped around to see a perfect Windsor knot. Then she looked up. Six feet three inches of gorgeous man smiled down at her. Her eyes widened to saucers. Soft brown eyes framed by long thick and curly lashes connected with hers. His warm brown cinnamon skin seemed to glow with added masculine virility. His features were chiseled to perfection.

Everything she saw from across the hall was now up close and personal—high cheekbones, strong, firm chin and, heaven help her, full, sexy, kissable lips. His smile broadened slowly, showing sparkling white teeth. An instant later Bonnie's words popped into her mind—*too, too sexy*. She opened her mouth to speak, but then closed it quickly. Her heart stuttered and it felt as if all the air in the room had been extinguished.

She tried to play off a polite smile, but she knew it was too late. Hearing his voice, smelling his cologne and seeing him this close to her had completely taken over her senses. Touching and tasting him were the two senses left. She had no idea how long Keith had been watching her, but she knew it was long enough.

"Hello," he said, extending his hand. "Keith Washington."

"Good afternoon, Mr. Washington," she said, surprised her voice was as calm even though her insides were a chaotic jumble of nerves. She quickly turned back around to focus on the discussion.

"And you are…"

"Gia Duncan," she said, still facing forward.

"Nice job, Gia Duncan," Keith said, then paused. "Almost."

"I beg your pardon…job?" she asked.

"Attack job," Keith clarified.

"No one here has been attacked that I'm aware of. The mayor is simply being held accountable for the promises he had made three and a half years ago."

"I don't have a lot of patience."

"That makes two of us," she snapped back.

He smirked. "Still, quite an impressive spectacle, Ms. Duncan," he said, then paused a moment. "Yours, I presume," he added, seeming to already know the answer

Gia glanced to the side but didn't turn around completely, nor did she reply. She hadn't expected to be found out so soon, and she certainly had no intention of out-and-out giving herself away. That would be too easy for him. She started looking for Bill. All of a sudden he was nowhere in sight.

"Actually, that was more of a statement than a question," he said. "This was quite obviously your handiwork, along with your suddenly absent friend, of course." She still didn't respond.

Someone excused themselves, then passed behind Keith, causing him to move forward closer to Gia. Their bodies were nearly connected. She felt the warmth of his close proximity. She took a deep breath and held her own. She had the courage and she had the determination. Now all she needed was the discipline to bide her time and let her organization do the work.

The questions for the mayor came in a bullet-riddled secession. The OCC participants she'd planted in the audience were relentless. They asked every question assigned and then added follow-up questions, as well. They followed one by one after each other like a tsunami. The audience was coming around to exactly what she had planned. It was perfect. By the fifth question, it was obvious that this wasn't going to be just another political lovefest for Blake Washington.

After a short time it wasn't just the OCC members asking pertinent questions. The rest of the audience joined in. The easy-breezy town hall meeting had turned into a serious question-and-answer accountability session. But they weren't just for Blake, they were for all the elected officials. The OCC was a sponsor and they wanted answers. She wanted answers, too.

To his credit, Blake was knowledgeable and on point. The questions came and he answered them with ease and at times appropriate levity. The charm was back. He never lost his composure. He was a trial lawyer and a politician. It wasn't that easy to rattle him.

Still, Gia glanced around the open hall smiling, nodding and very proud of herself. All eyes were focused on the mayor, intent on watching and listening to every word. He had everything under control.

"I think we're through here," Gia said, stealing a sideways glance, careful not to turn completely round.

"Are you sure?" Keith asked.

She turned completely around to him this time. "We made our point, proved our case."

"Are you sure?" he repeated.

He was testing her. She smiled knowingly. "Absolutely."

"I don't think you realize what you're up against," he said.

"I could say the same of you," she rebutted quickly. "The people want answers and results this time around. So, before we give your father another chance, he needs to show that he deserves it. And know that just giving lip service isn't going to do it."

"Lip service," he repeated, then licked his lips,

focusing on her mouth. "Would you like to elaborate on that terminology?"

She smiled in spite of herself. "You know exactly what I'm talking about, Mr. Washington."

"And am I to understand that you alone speak for all the people of Philadelphia?"

"I didn't say I did."

"You implied as much. Who exactly do you represent?"

"I work with the Organization for Community Change. We're nonprofit, so we don't answer to anyone except the people of Philadelphia."

Keith smiled. "That's very naïve of you."

Her anger instantly spiked. The audacity of his implication felt as if she'd been doused with ice water on a hot day. She was speechless. She released. "Maybe you think your charm and charisma can influence others, but I assure you, I'm not easily manipulated. Nor am I impressed. You got OCC's endorsement the last time, but these are different times. This city wants answers one way or another. So, Mr. Washington, I suggest you prepare your camp for the battle of your career."

"Once again, are you sure?" Keith asked. His tone was crisp and unyielding.

She smirked. "Very," she said definitively. "It would be a huge mistake to underestimate me." She turned back around.

"Thank you for the warning," he said, leaning in.

"Don't mention it," she shot over her shoulder.

Keith nodded, then focused on the assembly

again. A question was asked and after his father answered there was loud applause. Then he turned the questions around and asked the young woman what part of the city she was from. She stammered a few seconds, avoiding the question, and when pressed, she answered, stating that she was from Los Angeles and had just arrived the day before. The crowd laughed, booed her and she sat down, turning beet red.

The mayor went on to ask a few others who'd asked volatile questions where they were from. Most answered that they were from the suburbs. It was all over at that point, as the true Philadelphians grew openly hostile toward the outsiders and began yelling at them to sit down.

"You know this isn't over," Gia said over her shoulder.

"I'd be greatly disappointed if it was. It was a pleasure meeting you, Gia Duncan." Gia turned completely around to face him. "I guess the battle begins. Pity," Keith said, knowing that his father had the audience firmly back in his corner.

"Why a pity?" Gia asked.

"We could have been very good together," he said.

"Sorry, I already have a position."

"There are always new positions," he suggested.

"Yes, I'm sure there are," she confirmed.

Keith leaned in closer and looked down the length of her body. "But for the record—" he licked his full, kissable lips "—I wasn't talking about professionally."

The enticing sight sent a burning wave of heat straight down through the center of her body. All of a sudden Gia began to wonder. She opened her mouth and then closed it just as quickly. She understood exactly what he meant. She also understood that he was a lawyer and that meant he played games for a living. Fine, she could play, too. She boldly looked into his sexy eyes and then up and down his body. Then she smiled seductively and returned the favor by licking her lips, as well. "For the record, I agree. Pity."

She turned to walk away, but he spoke up quickly and quietly as he captured her hand. "You know," he began softly, then leaned in so as not to disturb the others standing nearby, "there's no reason why we can't still be friends through all this." He handed her his business card.

"Of course there is," she said, taking his card, looking at it. "But then again..." She smiled a crooked smile, handed him her card and then walked away.

Keith chuckled. The sound was deep, hearty and soulful. He nodded as he watched her go. As soon as she got to the exit, she turned and took one last look at him. He had stopped laughing and was now smiling at her. She nodded, turned and walked out.

It was obvious she had no idea what she was doing. This was his arena and he played for keeps. There was no way an amateur was going to outmaneuver him. Yeah, she took the first point, but this game went to the player who lasted the longest. He intended to win, by any means necessary.

A few minutes later Megan came over. "I know, I know. This is a public relations disaster. I'm on it," she said anxiously.

Keith was still smiling and holding Gia's business card. "No, not at all. I'll make a few phone calls. We'll be all good by the end of the day. But get me as much information as you can on OCC."

"Okay, I already spoke with Ms. Los Angeles. Her name's Simone Carpenter. She's an aspiring actress."

He chuckled. "Don't worry about her, she was just a distraction. I doubt she has much to do with this. Focus on compiling an OCC file. I want everything on them, starting from the top."

"I already have my team working on it," she said as she followed him back toward the side door. Her limber fingers sped rapidly across the tiny keys of her BlackBerry like lightning.

Moments later the program had begun to wind down. By the end, his father's applause had quickly turned into a whistling standing ovation. Keith was already making preemptive calls to the media, spinning a questionable story into pure gold.

Chapter 3

The meeting was over. Gia stepped outside and released the breath she'd been holding ever since she walked away from Keith Washington. Playing with fire was dangerous. Playing with Keith could be cataclysmic. She had no idea why she said what she had said to him. She'd been nonconfrontational all her life. It wasn't until she stepped up to her father and grandfather that she had actually spoken up for herself at all and didn't just go along with the status quo.

It was totally and completely out of character for her, but for some reason it felt right to step up to Keith Washington. He was flirting and she flirted right back. And even now her heart was pounding like a jackhammer, but she knew it was more about what would happen next. She was sure he wasn't the kind of man to just let a comment like hers rest.

"Oh, my God, that was insane," Bonnie said excitedly as soon as they left the main hall. "That was incredible. We totally rocked that. Seriously, we so need to celebrate right now. What do you think about Beluga caviar, escargot in butter and Perrier-Jouët champagne at Le Bec Fin on Rittenhouse Square?"

"That's a bit too extravagant."

"Okay, how about truffles, poached salmon and iced vodka at the Ritz?"

"How about we just order pizza and beer when we get back to the office?" Gia said as they walked through the throngs of people standing around outside as they both looked around for Bill. "There he is," Gia said, seeing Bill's car parked just down the street.

"Where? I don't see him," Bonnie said, looking around.

"There, on the corner of the next block. Let's go," she said.

A block away Bill sat in his car with the phone on speaker listening to Lester Jameson tear him apart. He rolled his eyes toward the tinted sunroof. Lester was stuck in a continuous loop of hysterics and high drama. This was the fourth time he repeated the same damn monologue. He wouldn't allow Bill to defend himself.

"Do you have any idea how badly this is going to come back on me? It looks like I planted them in the audience. The media's already castrating me on mudslinging and dirty politicking. I don't need any more of this kind of publicity."

Bill sighed heavily. This rampage had been going on for the last five minutes. Bill had already apologized profusely. "But how was I supposed to know he would ask them where they were from?"

"What are you, ten? This isn't a playground brawl. It's politics, buddy. This is hardball. You wanted to play in the big leagues, well, here you are. Step up to the plate."

"Lester, I'm sorry. It won't happen again. I promise. We'll regroup at Friday's press conference. I already have it all worked out. We'll be there and we'll be ready."

"Fine, just make sure that you have something to discredit Blake and that it won't come back to me. I've already got this corruption probe hanging over my head. And what about that endorsement you promised?"

"I'm working on it."

"Work faster. Election Day is in a few weeks. Remember, you don't get your position if I don't get the office."

"I know, I know."

There was a muffled sound in the background. Bill could hear someone questioning Lester. He answered by disavowing knowledge of the audience members and blaming the sponsors like OCC for distracting the public and clouding the true issues.

Bill slammed the palm of his hand on the steering wheel. He had not intended for this to come back on OCC. And here Lester was, serving them up on a platter.

Bill saw two more news vans pull up. He looked in the rearview mirror. He knew this was going to get real crazy real soon. People were starting to mingle around outside. Then he spotted Bonnie and Gia walking down the street toward his car.

"Get it done," Lester said, getting back to Bill.

"You just gave us up," Bill said in a restrained tone.

"It's politics, boy—better you than me." The line went dead.

A few seconds later his cell phone rang again. He answered. It was Linda, one of the OCC office staff. Apparently the phones had been ringing off the hook. News agencies were desperate for an interview with the organization. "All right, don't say anything. Just get their contact information and wait until we get there," he said. He was still talking to the assistant when Gia and Bonnie got into the car.

"Hey," Gia said as she sat down in the front seat, "so, what happened to you? You disappeared on us."

"I was there for most of it. I left to get an early start to the car. So, how was the ending?"

"Not as good as it began," Gia said.

Bonnie chuckled. "That's an understatement. The mayor started going back at the OCC people, asking where we lived, and one of the women *you* hired actually said that she lived in Los Angeles. Can you believe that? Everybody started laughing and that was it. It was all downhill after that, if you ask my opinion. "

"Nobody asked your opinion, Bonnie," Bill said gruffly.

"No, she's right. Who was she?" Gia interrupted.

"Seriously, that was the dumbest thing I ever heard," Bonnie said. "Why would you say you're from California at a Philadelphia town hall meeting? That's just stupid."

Bill glared at Bonnie in the rearview mirror.

"Bill, who was she? She obviously isn't part of OCC, and I've never seen her as a volunteer."

"She's a friend. She wanted to help."

"And what was with all the makeup and weaved-in blond hair? She looked ridiculous."

"Bonnie," Gia said.

"Why don't you shut up?" Bill insisted.

"Why don't you?" Bonnie snapped back.

Gia shook her head. It was obvious this was going to turn into another one of the usual brother-versus-sister battles. For some reason Bill did not get along with his half sister, Bonnie, even though she adored him. Gia had a feeling it was because she still had money whereas he'd blown through his inheritance and trust fund in less than three years. Now he was essentially broke. Either way, she didn't want to hear any more. She reached over and turned on the radio. The news station came on midway into a news report.

"...in this hour's top story, it looks like Mayor Blake Washington got himself in a bit of a tight squeeze at the North Field Community Center this afternoon. He was hammered on all sides today by members of the Organization for Community Change. Since Julia Duncan's stroke three months

ago, it looks like the organization is back stronger than ever and they've set their sights on Mayor Blake Washington. I have a feeling we're gonna hear more from them in the future."

"You bet you are," Gia said, knowing her grandmother would be too pleased about today. "Did you hear that—we got major airtime? That's fantastic!" Gia said excitedly. She couldn't stop smiling and her heart was beating like crazy. She would still be feeling the high of besting Blake Washington on a political level at least for a while. "I can't believe how great that felt. We did it. We did it."

"Yeah, we did it," Bill said calmly.

"And that was only the beginning. We're gonna get changes made. OCC is gonna hold Philadelphia politicians accountable. If they want to win elections, they're gonna have to step up and work for the people and not just big businesses and their political lobbyists."

"So, overall, what did you think of him?" Bill asked as he pulled to a stop at a traffic light.

"He was an impressive speaker," Gia said.

"Well, I thought he was fantastic," Bonnie added.

Bill glanced up in the rearview mirror again. He frowned disgustedly, not expecting his sister to add anything more to the conversation from the backseat. "Is that all, just impressive?" he asked Gia.

"He's also charming and intelligent. Shall I go on?" she asked.

"Now, we are talking about Blake Washington, right?" Bill said.

"Yes, of course. Why? Who else would we be talking about?"

"Well, the way you and Keith were talking and looking at each other seemed and looked a little suspect," he said with a sideways taunt. "What I mean is, it looked like the two of you were about to get *chummy*."

"Chummy? I have no idea what you're talking about," Gia said, then turned and looked out the side window dismissively seeing the streets of Philadelphia pass by. Bonnie plugged her earbuds into her ears and Bill was lost in his thoughts as the news report continued with sports, weather and then more local news.

Unlike for most in the OCC, this wasn't her adopted city. She was born and raised and had lived in Philly with her mother and father until the age of ten. She remembered it well. Her parents divorced and there was a long ugly battle over her future. The courts, presumably with her grandfather's collaboration, awarded her father full custody. Her mother had a nervous breakdown and was hospitalized and a year later when her father remarried she was sent away to a boarding school in Boston. And that was the beginning of her real life. Both college and grad school were spent in Boston. Afterward she was expected to return to Philadelphia and go to work in the family business making money and carry on the Duncan family name with a family friend's rich son or grandson.

That was their idea of her perfectly planned out

life. Fortunately it wasn't hers. After college she refused everything. Her father and grandfather were
furious. They threatened to take her trust fund and
inheritance and she gladly volunteered it. They were
stunned; she was overjoyed. Happily for her, greed
and self-indulged arrogance aren't hereditary.

She could still see their faces when she turned
her back and walked out on everything. Priceless.
She smiled to herself even now, years later. It was
the best day of her life because she made her mother
and grandmother proud.

They drove past a campaign billboard of Blake
Washington. He was smiling and she instantly
thought about a six-foot-three-inch gorgeous man
named Keith. She bit her lower lip, thinking about
the last thing she had said to him. It was challenging and provocative. She knew she opened up the
possibility of something more between them. She
had no idea why she said it. It was pure impetuous
impulse. But chances were he wouldn't do anything
about it—thank goodness for that.

Keith stood just outside the North Field Community Center waiting for his father to come out.
He smiled, shook hands and even answered a few
sound-bite questions about the town meeting for the
local news. Twenty minutes later Blake came out of
the building. His friend Ace Miller walked out with
him along with a news team and eight or so others.
After a few more handshakes, photo-ops and waves,
they got in the car and drove off back to Center City.

"Do you have any idea what that was?" Keith said as soon as the car drove away.

"That was desperate politics," Blake said.

"Miller has some serious explaining to do."

"No, Ace didn't know. He had nothing to do with what happened in there. Believe me, it was just as much a surprise to him as it was to us. He's furious. He feels they used and besmirched the community center. I had to stop him from throwing the whole OCC crew out."

"OCC," Keith repeated slowly, "since when do they openly confront politicians in a public forum like that? They're primarily letter-writing pacifists."

"Looks like the game players are trying to change the rules."

"Yes, it does," Keith said, and nodded. "And we're not going to be caught short and exposed like that again. I want to know exactly what they're up to. I already have Megan getting more information on them."

"Or you could just ask your great-aunt about them."

"Mamma Lou, why, what do you mean?"

"She was there at the beginning. Your grandmother was one of the founding members of OCC along with Julia Banks."

"When was this?"

"This was back in the early and mid-seventies, I believe."

"I didn't know that," Keith said.

"Oh, yes, your grandmother and great-aunt were

very political in their day. They were considered
quite radical by their parents and friends. They belonged to the Southern Christian Leadership Conference. They organized and held numerous sit-ins
and protests here in the city during the Civil Rights
Movement. They marched on Washington in sixty-
three and rode to the Deep South on Freedom Ride
buses to register voters and protect against discrim-
ination and segregation. They were even arrested a
few times for civil disobedience. That's what made
me want to get into politics in the first place. They
knew there was a better way. They wanted change
and a better life for the future. The OCC was founded
on the premise of it."

Keith smiled. Learning the beginnings of OCC
might be helpful. And since he'd lost the challenge
with his brothers, distracting Mamma Lou with OCC
might be a good way to keep her too distracted to
meddle in his personal life. "So Mamma Lou married and went to live in Virginia and then Grandmom
died. I presume Julia Banks just continued the OCC
premise alone, so how did it go from making community changes to a political watchdog?"

"That, you're gonna have to ask your great-aunt
when she gets here. She's the only one who would
know now except, of course, Julia Banks," Blake said
just as the car pulled up in front of the Washington
& Associates Law Firm office building.

Keith opened the door and got out, then turned
back to his father. "Dad, don't forget you're meeting

with the teachers union to get their endorsement this evening. I'll meet you there at six."

"Why don't you take the evening off? Your mother's meeting me at the union hall and then we're going to dinner with some friends. You've been working too hard lately. Carrying your legal clients plus managing my reelection is above and beyond. I'm sure your mother and I can handle it alone this evening. Go home and get some rest."

"I'm fine. I'll meet you—"

"Keith, that wasn't a suggestion," Blake said firmly.

"Dad, after what happened this afternoon I think I need to be there this evening. It's the perfect opportunity for OCC and every other obstructive organization to push into the limelight to get media attention. Fifteen minutes of fame is all they want. And after today all bets are off."

"If that's the case, then there's nothing much we can do. The freedom of the press works for everyone."

"I'm not concerned about everyone right now. I already beefed up security for the remainder of your personal appearances, including press conferences."

Blake nodded. "Do what you need to do, but still take the evening off—no arguments."

Keith nodded. "Okay, I will. I have a few things to catch up on at the office. Call me if you change your mind. Thanks for the ride." He closed the door and watched the car drive off down the street. A few seconds later he breezed through the main lobby and headed up to the top-floor law offices.

Megan, while still texting on her cell phone, met him as soon as he stepped off the elevator. "Hey, I just spoke with the governor's aide. We've confirmed. He'll be in the city next week and he wants to get together with the mayor and give his official endorsement," she said.

"Good, that'll work," Keith said as he walked past the reception area and down the hall toward his office, "but not at an official press conference. Let's find a venue that's more informal."

Megan nodded and followed Keith while still texting on her cell phone. Kate, Keith's administrative assistant and the office's senior manager, followed close behind with her computer pad in her hands. "Keith, you have a teleconferencing meeting in half an hour with Senator Kingsley. Your mail is on your desk and the contracts you were expecting just arrived," she said, handing him an unopened overnight express package.

"Thanks," Keith said, taking the package, "and, Kate, I need you to get my mother on the phone. I'm working here late this evening. She may be in court. If so, leave a message for her to call me when she's free. Also, I need you to pull a few hard-copy files before you head out. Check my email in-box for the list."

She nodded, turned and went back to her desk. Keith and Megan continued into his office. "Okay, I have that information you wanted on OCC," Megan said. "It's not complete, but it'll give you an idea of what we're up against."

"Let's hear what you have," he said, sitting at his desk and opening his laptop.

"Okay, Organization of Community Change, OCC, is a nonprofit. According to the information I have so far, and from their website, it was organized in the late seventies to bring attention to the political corruption and unlawful police brutality stemming from the Powelton Village incident. From there it grew into a political action and community service organization. Julia Banks was the primary listed until three years ago when her granddaughter took over.

"The organization became more focused on political policy and eliminating political corruption during the last administration. They took an aggressive stance and led the recall. They are also noted as being responsible for outing a few political figures in the eighties and nineties. Their endorsement can carry a lot of weight in some circles. The older constituents still rely heavily on them. Right now they're critical of the mayor. We could use a bump in the polls, and they could give it to us."

"I agree. We need to connect with them. No, I need to connect with them. I want you to follow the money trail. Who are their leading contributors?" he asked, pulling the tab from the overnight express package and taking out several contracts.

"Their main funding is unknown and I haven't been able to track it so far. But they get a considerable amount from the Emma Washington Foundation headed by—"

"Louise Gates."

Megan looked up from her computer pad. "Yeah, that's right, your grandmother and her older sister."

"Tell me about Julia Banks's daughter."

"Audrey Duncan grew up lower middle class and married rich. She had one daughter out of wedlock, Gia Duncan. The birth certificate lists Gia's father's name as Samuel Duncan of Duncan Real Estate Development. Audrey and Samuel married later. She died of bronchial pneumonia and myocardial fibrosis when Gia was twelve. Gia was at the community center today."

"Wait, Samuel Duncan is Gia Duncan's father?" he questioned. Megan nodded. "So that means Lawrence Duncan is her—"

"Yes, Lawrence Duncan, who owns almost an eighth of the city's prime real estate, is Gia's paternal grandfather."

Keith nodded, smiling. "Interesting, she's got some serious money behind her. So that's her unknown funding."

"Actually, I'm not sure about that part. Rumor has it there was some kind of family feud a few years ago and she was cut off."

"There's cut off and then there's cut off. What about Julia?"

She nodded. "Julia Banks had a major heart attack three years ago. That's when Gia moved here from Boston and took over. Then six months ago she had a stroke. She's currently in a nursing home in west Philly. Gia Duncan is heading the OCC with her lead associate, William B. Axelby the Third. There are also a number of lower-level associates, including Axelby's half sister, Bonnie. OCC's main focus and objective is to hold accountable the procedures and practices of local politicians and to…"

Keith continued listening as he read through emails and updated his father's planner for the following day. He cleared the morning for last-minute news feeds, an online video promo he planned and any Q&A from local news agencies. He didn't have to do any major damage control since the OCC had basically shot themselves in the foot with the last few questioners, but he needed to be ready for the next time. They'd tipped their hand too soon. Now he knew exactly what to expect.

"Dating…single and lives on—"

"Hold up, hold up, stop," Keith said, paying attention again. "Go back."

"As for Gia Duncan's personal life, she dated a stockbroker, before that a businessman, both very wealthy. Before that she dated a lawyer who turned out to be married. She ended it when she found out. It doesn't look like she's dated at all since she's been here in Philly."

"She hasn't dated in three years?" he questioned.

"No, no one we can find. All she does now is work twenty-four-seven."

"Sounds like she needs some excitement in her

life. I think that's my in," Keith said, smiling, knowing the exact approach he'd take. "What else?"

"She's twenty-eight, single and lives on Delaware Avenue—actually not too far from your city apartment. She went to boarding school, college and grad school in Boston, then returned to the area to work with her grandmother at OCC three years ago. She has a law degree from Harvard and was top of her class in the LLM Masters of Law Program with a focus on human rights."

"Harvard LLM, impressive. So she's a lawyer," Keith said as he went through the contracts in the package.

"Yes, she was in Boston, but she obviously doesn't practice now. As a matter of fact, the OCC has used this law firm several times in the last few years."

"Used us?" he questioned. Megan nodded. "Assigned to whom?"

She shook her head. "Closed records. It doesn't say."

Keith's private office phone rang. Megan stopped reading as soon as he answered. It was his secretary informing him that his mother was headed back to court and would call him back later. "Megan, we'll finish this up later. Send me what you have." She nodded, got up and walked out.

Keith sat at his desk a few moments thinking about the events of the day. Gia's last comment in particular made him smile. He shook his head, intrigued. She had no idea what she'd started.

He had felt the burn instantly, and her crooked

little sexy smile sealed his interest. He opened the file his associate had emailed him and read through it quickly. She was still working on it, but what she'd sent him so far made him even more curious. She was a Duncan and that meant deep pockets. She was the only granddaughter of Lawrence Duncan and that meant power. He wondered what a presumably wealthy woman, as Gia obviously was, would be doing in a nonprofit organization policing politicians. There had to be something more to this.

Seeing the OCC's phone number, he opened his cell phone, then closed it and smiled. Just calling OCC wasn't the definite impact he wanted to make. His smiled broadened. Showing up in their office was. He chuckled to himself, closed his laptop, got up and headed to the office door. He stopped at Kate's desk. She looked up as he approached. "Kate, check with the firm's records. I need to know who handled the OCC account. I'm not sure when."

"It was three years ago. Drew caught the case."

Keith smiled. He should have known that Kate would know. When it came to the law practice, she knew everything. "Thanks. Is Drew in today?"

"Yes, he should be in his office."

"Let me know when the conference call is ready. I'll be with Drew."

She nodded. "I'll have those files pulled," she said.

"Thanks," Keith said, turning and headed toward his brother's office a few doors down. He knocked at the slightly cracked door. He opened it a bit more and stepped inside. Drew was on the phone. He looked up, saw his brother and motioned for him to come in. Keith walked in as Drew ended his phone call.

He grabbed the remote control and turned the sound up on the TV across from his desk. "Hey, what happened today? Dad's all over the news."

"An unfortunate miscalculation of intent," Keith said, sitting down in the seat across from the desk. "We were upstaged by a few members of a group called OCC. But Dad handled it admirably as usual and came out on top."

"Organization for Community Change," Drew said.

"You worked with them?" Keith asked.

"Yeah, I did a few pro bono jobs for them a few years ago. I worked with Julia Banks. I understand she had a stroke a while back. I heard that her granddaughter's taking over."

"She has. What do you know about her?"

"Not much. She wasn't around a lot at the time. It was during her move down from Boston. I know she's attractive, intelligent, distant and a half minute from being openly hostile."

"What do you mean?"

"I mean she has a chip on her shoulder that's the size of a giant sequoia."

"Why's that?"

Drew shrugged. "I don't have a clue. I assumed it had something to do with her father and grandfather. I heard they disowned her since she didn't go into the family business."

Keith smiled. "So she chose working with her

grandmother at a nonprofit over making millions with Dad and Granddad."

There was a knock on Drew's office door and then it opened. Kate poked her head inside. "Keith, your conference call will begin in four minutes."

"Thanks, Kate, I'll be right there."

She nodded and left. Keith looked across at Drew. "I think Gia was the mastermind behind this afternoon's sideshow."

"What are you gonna do?" Drew asked.

"Get them out of the way until after the election."

"How?"

"I have a few ideas. Either way, I think it's time Gia and I got better acquainted," Keith said, standing to leave. "Oh, any words on the arrival date?"

"No. Jeremy and I were just talking about that. Neither of us has heard anything. We were thinking it was a false alarm. Maybe she's not coming."

Keith shook his head. "Nah, she's coming. The question is when."

"You're that sure?" Drew asked. Keith nodded. "Okay, I'll be at the courthouse in a few hours. I'll try to catch up with Mom and see if she knows anything. Either way I'll let you know what I find out."

Keith nodded again. "Good, I'll talk to you later."

Drew chuckled and shook his head. "Hey, good luck with OCC. I have a feeling you're gonna need it."

Keith waved his hand as he walked out the door. He knew he didn't need luck. She was a woman and that's all he needed.

Chapter 4

Gia placed her elbows on her desk and rubbed her temples. Her head was pounding. The headache she had felt coming earlier was now here. It had been a long day and right now all she wanted to do was lie down, close her eyes and rest, but she knew she couldn't. She'd made a dozen calls and was now waiting to get information in order to plan the organization's next move.

"Hey, are you coming back out to the party?" Bonnie asked as she walked into Gia's office.

"Yeah, I'll be there in a few minutes," Gia said without bothering to look up.

"You okay?"

"Yeah, fine, just a little headache. I'll be right there." Bonnie nodded and left. Fifteen minutes later

Gia was still sitting at the desk in her office. Now the television was turned on and she was watching the latest news report. An ice-cold half-eaten slice of pizza on a white paper plate sat in front of her. She glanced at it and crinkled her nose, then picked up the bottle of water, forgetting she'd emptied it an hour ago.

Optimistically, she'd watched the news reports over and over again. Of course nothing ever changed. They all rolled the same footage repeatedly, and each time she hoped to see something different. She didn't. She grabbed the remote control and changed channels—more of the same.

She took a deep satisfied breath and decided that by all accounts it was a good day. She'd succeeded and done exactly what she intended—she got OCC noticed. They had had their fifteen minutes of fame and now she needed to make sure they stayed in the spotlight, front and center. People were interested and the office phones had been ringing all evening. They'd made their point and they planted the idea that the people of Philadelphia needed and deserved more than lip service and politics as usual from their mayor and city council members.

The news report continued with Keith Washington standing outside the community center. A reporter asked him a question about OCC and what had happened inside. His answer was respectfully dismissive of OCC while still on point with his father's campaign message. The reporter's eyes seemed to haze over as she smiled up at him. It was exactly as she expected—after all, he was a lawyer and a Washington. His charm and charisma sparkled right through the television. Gia wondered how long it would be before he threw his hat in the political ring. The crowd around him cheered and she knew right then she would be taking on two consummate professionals, father and son.

She heard a cheer and applause from the front, then looked up at the slightly cracked office door. She could see that a few of the organization's volunteers were still there even though the main celebration had long since wound down and most volunteers were already gone.

A news clip of Keith speaking repeated on a different channel. She muted the volume and just watched his face as he spoke. He was everything any woman could want, beautiful white teeth, long dark lashes, dark sexy eyes and lips that could very likely send a woman through the roof. Yep, Bonnie was right, he was gorgeous. Everything about him screamed *sexy*. And right now having a little sexy in her dull, boring life wouldn't be such a bad thing.

She couldn't remember the last time she'd had a date or had even gone out to have fun, for that matter. Like with her grandmother, the OCC had taken up all of her life. She'd pushed everything back for the greater good and right now that greater good was holding Blake Washington accountable to his constituents. Her thoughts eased back to Keith and his broad shoulders, sexy smile and gorgeous eyes. She wondered what it would be like to be with him.

She reached over and picked up an envelope on her desk. It was an invitation to the mayor's Initiative Conference. It had come two weeks ago. With everything going on, she had completely forgotten about it. It was a new program that was started by the mayor's office three years ago. The OCC had never once been invited. Now they had. She originally had declared she was going, but now she wasn't sure. But seeing Keith once again might be interesting.

She opened her laptop and RSVP'd the invitation. Then she typed in Keith's name and added the Washington & Associates Law Firm of Philadelphia for clarification. His profile came up along with a few thousand other hits. She clicked on the Wikipedia hit and waited a split second to see everything there was to know about his life. He was born in Philadelphia. He was a few years older than she was and he practiced legislative and regulatory law, specializing in politics. He had represented numerous politicians and stood before the Supreme Court. The more she read, the more impressive he appeared.

Then curiously, she checked out the images tab, seeing Keith photographed with numerous people, senators, military people, businessmen and of course women—lots of women. All were beautifully stunning in gowns, suits, dresses and even a few in bathing suits. Some of them she recognized as models and actresses.

"Hey," Bill said quickly as he poked his head into her office. Gia jumped like a kid with her hand caught in the cookie jar. "You all right?" he asked.

She nodded. "Yeah, just a headache, what's up?"

"I'm headed out. Remember, I have that interview taping in the morning. And just to let you know we're all set for the press conference Friday at City Hall."

"Wait, I need to talk to you about that," she said, closing her laptop and turning the television off.

He stopped. "What about it?" he asked.

"We have to regroup. We can't just show up and do what we did today. It's a press conference and I'm sure they've tightened security. It worked this afternoon because we sponsored the event and were afforded the element of surprise, but I don't see that happening again."

"And that's exactly why it will work. They won't expect it."

Gia shook her head, disagreeing. "No. I spoke with Keith Washington. He's no fool. We just can't walk into a closed press conference without media credentials and start asking questions."

"Wait, you spoke with Keith Washington about what?"

"What do you think? About the town hall meeting, of course."

"So you told him it was us," Bill said disappointedly.

"No, of course not, I didn't have to, he told me."

"What do you mean he told you? How did he

know it was us? You must have said something to him. He couldn't just know without being told."

"I don't see why not. He's an intelligent and perceptive man."

"It sounds like you actually admire him."

The day had been one trying irritation after another. She'd been confronted by Keith Washington and now she was being interrogated by Bill. Enough was enough. "Look, like I said, the man is no fool. We're not going to do it. If we do, we'll be put out and that's not something I want on our record. Who'll take us seriously then?"

"If we're put out, then it'll show that Blake Washington has something to hide. We're in a win-win scenario."

"No, we'll look like radical fools. That's not us."

"Gia, I think you're giving Washington too much credit. He's not going to be paying attention to us. We're probably off his radar already. That's how these political handlers work."

"He's not just a political handler," she warned, "he's *the* political handler and his main focus is his father."

Bill shook his head. "Wow, he really got to you, didn't he?"

"Nobody got to me, Bill. Attending the press conference isn't a rational course of action at this time. We'll pass."

"Listen, trust me on this. This was my idea, my plan, so I know it'll work. They only look at the big picture. He doesn't care about us. We're just a blip on the radar to them. I wouldn't worry about Friday. We'll stick to our original plan and go. Did you check out the newscasts earlier?" Gia nodded. "He totally dismissed us when asked."

"Sure, on-camera he dismissed us, but what about off-camera? No, I disagree. If we go out there tomorrow it'll be an embarrassment. We'll be totally ridiculed and lose everything we've gained so far."

"Gia, I've been doing this a lot longer than you have," Bill said, using the argument he always used when he wanted his way. In truth, her grandmother had brought him on board just a few months before she joined. "We'll go and state our case and ask the pertinent questions no one else wants to ask. Then Blake Washington will come knocking on that door looking to make a deal."

As if on cue, there was a knock on the door. "Yes," Gia said.

Bonnie opened the door and poked her head into the office. "Hey," she began happily, "y'all are missing out on all the fun. Come on out and enjoy."

"I'll be there in a minute," Gia said, smiling. Bonnie nodded and then left. Gia knew everyone needed this. They worked long, hard hours sending letters, emails and making phone calls. They were dedicated and focused volunteers. There weren't being paid, so a small celebratory party wasn't too much to expect. It was the first real release in a long time.

"I gotta go," Bill said with his hand already on the doorknob. "Trust me, it'll be fine."

"I disagree." Gia knew a power play when she heard one. Bill always thought that her grandmother should have left him in charge, and maybe on some level she did, too. But she didn't. She gave the reins to Gia, and she was going to do exactly as her grandmother planned—take charge. "We're not going—end of discussion."

Bill held his hands up in surrender. "Okay, fine, whatever. I gotta go." He walked out.

Suddenly, she still felt the shadow of doubt. Bill was underestimating Keith, and his dismissive misjudgment could undermine everything her grandmother had built over the years. She stood up and walked out into the outer office.

There were only five volunteers left after a roomful earlier. They all looked up as soon as she came out. They started clapping and cheering. "Okay, okay, listen, I just wanted to thank you all again. You did a phenomenal job today. Thank you so much. I'm sure my grandmother would be very proud of us," Gia spoke over the noise. Everyone applauded again. "That said, we're gonna pass on going to the press conference this Friday."

They all looked at each other and then back to her. She could see the questions in their eyes. "I know, I know. We've been planning this back-to-back second appearance for weeks, but I think they're gonna be ready for us this time."

"What does Bill say?" someone asked.

Gia glanced at the man who spoke. Although he didn't come around often, she knew him well. His name was Danny Mead. He had a relatively popular political blog and touted his conspiracy ideas and opinions to anyone who'd listen. He was also a brown-nosing kiss-up, particularly when it came to anyone with money. He probably thought that since her grandmother didn't have big money, she didn't either. She let him believe it. "Bill disagrees with me. But since this is my call and I have final say, we're gonna pass."

"Are you sure that's the right course to take? Maybe you should change your mind and listen to Bill. I mean, no offense or anything, but he must know what he's talking about. I mean, all this was his idea." Danny spoke up, obviously enjoying the fact that he was taking center stage.

Everyone looked at him. "You obviously haven't been here long, Danny, or you would know all this was not Bill's idea. He just works here just like everyone else."

Gia smiled as everyone in the room looked from her to Danny. He didn't respond again. But a muscle in his neck twitched. She had shut him up. She knew he was testing her. He was the type, arrogant and chauvinistic. He pushed up at her and she was in the perfect frame of mind to put him in his place.

Bonnie smiled. "Okay, then what's next on the agenda?"

"The governor is coming into the city next week. He's expected to give Blake Washington his endorsement. I doubt the mayor's gonna want to have another town meeting, and that means he'll probably do it someplace less ceremonious. First thing tomorrow morning we need to find out where and when, then be there and be ready. But for right now, how about another slice of pizza?"

The room cheered and applauded. Bonnie opened the pizza box and placed a cold slice of pepperoni pizza on a paper plate and handed it to Gia. She took one bite and joined in the fun, staying about ten minutes. Then someone suggested they take the party to a nearby restaurant. Everyone quickly agreed and began cleaning up for the next day. Gia declined, then went back to her office. She sat down and tossed yet another slice of cold pizza on her desk.

A few minutes later Bonnie came barging into the office. "Oh, my God, Gia, you are never gonna believe who just walked into the front office," Bonnie said excitedly. "Guess, guess, come on, guess. You are never gonna guess. I swear, never."

"Who is it, Bonnie?" Gia asked dryly.

Bonnie's eyes sparkled. "Keith Washington."

Gia looked up. "What?"

"I know, I can't believe it," Bonnie said.

"He's here, right now in the office?" Gia clarified.

Bonnie nodded nonstop and nearly squealed. "Yeah, he is. How crazy is that? He's outside talking to the others."

Danny came up behind Bonnie. "What's he doing here? Did you call him? What does he want with you?"

Gia ignored Danny's questions. She was too busy trying to get her senses back. Her stomach dropped as if she'd just fallen from the roof of the Empire State Building. Her heart began to race and her hands shook. She stood up and looked around the office, seeing everything perfectly in place. "Okay, fine, ask him to come in," she said, faking calm. Bonnie nodded and hurried back to the front. A few seconds later he knocked on the open door and stepped aside smiling.

Keith Washington stood in the doorway of her office looking exactly as he had looked a few hours ago. Gia walked over. "Mr. Washington, good evening, please come in."

"Ms. Duncan," he said, extending his hand to shake. "Thank you for seeing me without an appointment. I usually don't just barge in like this. I hope I'm not disturbing you too much."

"No, not at all, have a seat," she said as she went back to stand behind her desk. He remained standing.

"I apologize for the lateness of the hour. I won't take up much of your time."

"What can I do for you, Mr. Washington?"

"First of all, you can call me Keith, please," he requested. She nodded. "I'll get right to the point. I'd like to facilitate an open dialogue with the mayor's office as I have done with a number of other city-wide community organizations."

"That would be acceptable," she said.

"Good. I'll have my assistant contact you in the next few days," he said, turning to leave.

She knew she should have just let him walk out, but she couldn't. "You know the people of this city expected great things from the mayor and city council on all levels. Your father made a number of generous promises regarding housing, education and a comprehensive jobs plan initiative. Now three and a half years later he wants us to give him more time to ignore every one of his erroneous promises again. I don't think so. Not this time."

Keith stopped and turned back to her. "First of all, Ms. Duncan, you need to read not only transcripts of the mayor's speeches, but also your own literature. OCC has backed Blake Washington both as city council member and mayor for the last ten years. And believe me when I say he does not make erroneous promises. You need to check your facts. Understand this, the mayor's one and only concern is to help this city and further its economic growth."

She nodded. "To play devil's advocate, perhaps that can best be accomplished by a new mayor in the office."

"You mean like Lester Jameson?" Keith asked.

"Hypothetically, yes. He has a reputation for helping the people."

"If you say so. I'm sure you of all people would know best."

"What's that supposed to mean?"

"Everyone knows that Lester Jameson has OCC in his pocket, and your attempt to discredit the mayor is in fact—"

"Whoa, first of all, OCC is in no one's pocket and secondly, we didn't discredit anyone," she quickly interrupted.

"At least the second part of that statement is true. You didn't damage the mayor, but you did call into question the reputation of your organization."

She opened her mouth, stunned by his audacity. Then she smiled knowingly. "You're a sore loser. Get over it. You got beat down today. Live with it."

Keith shook his head and looked around the small office. "Not necessarily. It was a rookie mistake and perhaps you need to know me better to understand the way I work. I'm very good at my job. By tomorrow morning the media will be questioning your organization, particularly centering on your very generous gift to us."

"What gift? We didn't give you any money," she declared immediately, thinking he'd pulled some underhanded ruse with fake bank statements sent to the media.

"No, not money, the nice lady from Los Angeles. Big mistake."

"I have no idea what you're talking about," she lied badly.

Keith saw it instantly. "Good, I'm glad to see it bothers you to lie. But the fact is, someone put 'the people' up to that shambles of a drive-by media assault this afternoon and—"

"What happened this afternoon was a fair political debate about issues, not a media assault," she interrupted.

"Including your actor friend from L.A.?" he questioned.

Gia took a deep breath, then hesitated. "As I said earlier, I have no idea about that. She's not an OCC volunteer."

Keith smirked. "Of course she isn't. I'd disavow her too if I were you, but a word to the wise, you might want to find out exactly who she is before casting stones. But I didn't come here to talk about your volunteers, paid or otherwise."

"We don't have to pay people to disagree with the mayor. Perhaps you're too far up in your ivory tower living in the lap of luxury to hear this, but news flash, Mr. Washington, people are suffering. They need jobs, affordable housing and education. Turning a blind eye to that and living in a privileged status isn't gonna fly anymore. The mayor promised us relief. Where is it?"

The fire in her eyes sparkled. Keith smiled. "You are beautiful when you're angry."

"Don't patronize me," she said, hearing the familiar vibration of her cell phone's message alert. She grabbed her purse and pulled it out, realizing she had never turned the ringer back on after she switched it to vibrate during the town hall meeting.

"Sorry, no, of course not," he said, "I apologize if you took it that way. If you felt insulted or patronized, it was unintended. In other words, I was joking."

"I don't joke," she said as she scrolled her caller ID, checking the last few missed calls.

"Yes, I can see that."

"Getting back to your original point, I accept your proposal to open a dialogue, but I don't think it's a good idea to..." She stopped talking on seeing a missed call from Crestar Nursing and Rehab Center. "Mr. Washington, we're gonna have to cut this short," she said, standing. "Thank you for stopping by this evening. I look forward to meeting with you in the next few days."

"Are you okay?" he asked. "You seem..."

"I'm fine, thank you. I just have to be someplace right now. I'd appreciate it if you'd have your assistant contact the office for an appointment next time. Good night." She held her hand out to shake.

He took her hand gently and felt a slight tremor. She quickly released his hand and walked to the door.

Keith nodded. "Good night." He left.

Gia hurried back to her desk, grabbed her cell phone and called the nursing home. An attendant at the nurse's station answered. "Hello, my name is Gia Duncan. I just got a message about my grandmother, Ms. Julia Banks," she said anxiously.

"Yes, Ms. Duncan, I called you earlier. Your grandmother's sleeping right now. There was an accident earlier and we're instructed to call a contact person if there's an incident. Ms. Banks stumbled and fell a few hours ago. She was attended to by our staff physician and then was taken to the emergency ward for precautionary treatment."

Gia's heart fell. "Did she have another stroke?"

"I can't say. The doctors had several tests done, including X-rays. They didn't find any broken or fractured bones. However, she did suffer a slight wrist sprain. It's wrapped and she's wearing a sling. She was returned to her room and is resting quietly."

Gia's heart quickened and beat like a snare drum. "Thank you. I'll be right there," she said, then ended the call and began gathering her things. She hurried out of her office, seeing that Bonnie and Danny were the only ones left in the front office. They had their coats on and were obviously leaving when she approached.

"Perfect timing, we were just on our way out," Bonnie said. "Oh, my God, I still can't believe Keith Washington just showed up like that. Can you believe it?"

"He was obviously sizing us up," Danny said suspiciously. "What did you two talk about?" he asked, expecting an answer.

Gia looked at Bonnie, ignoring Danny's comment. "I have to go."

"Everything okay?" Bonnie asked.

"I don't know yet. The nursing home called. There was an incident. I'm on my way there now. I'll call you in the morning," Gia said as she turned the lights off and followed Danny and Bonnie out the front door. Everyone disbursed to their separate cars. Gia hurried to her car and quickly drove off.

Keith, a few blocks away, slowed at a traffic light and then stopped at the intersection. Traffic was relatively light for this time of night. He hit the button on the steering wheel to turn on his music. Seconds later the mellow vocals of an old Marvin Gaye and Tammi Terell song played. He smiled and then chuckled to himself, remembering his mother and father performing the same selection at a family barbecue a few months earlier.

He glanced up in the rearview mirror, because he saw the brightness of two headlights rapidly coming up behind him. The car quickly veered to the right, pulling up beside him, and then stopped short. He glanced over to see Gia behind the wheel. She looked anxious, tapping her hands on the steering wheel and intently focused on the traffic light. He frowned. He knew her anxious behavior had something to do with the phone message she'd gotten. She'd been acting nervous since she glanced at her cell phone.

A few seconds later the light changed and she quickly turned the corner and sped off. Keith looked straight ahead and then at the corner Gia had just turned. He knew following her wasn't a good idea. It was intrusive and he knew it would look bad if she found out, but he also knew he didn't have much choice. He needed to know her deal. Curiously, he followed.

She didn't break any traffic laws, but she certainly bent a few as she drove with definite intent. He lost her briefly a couple of times, and then he saw her as she quickly turned a corner a block ahead. He turned to follow, but then her car was nowhere in sight. He slowly drove down the narrow cobblestone street, then stopped, seeing a well-lit sign on the corner. It read Crestar Medical Center.

He turned in, driving up the path, then caught a quick glimpse of her car driving around the side of the building. There was another sign, the Crestar Nursing and Rehab Center. He continued up a secluded driveway, then stopped upon seeing Gia get out of her car and hurry into the main building.

He parked and followed her inside.

Chapter 5

An hour and a half later, Gia paused just outside her grandmother's door. She leaned back against the whitewashed wall and looked down the empty hallway. It was late and certainly most of the patients were already asleep. A dim light from the nurse's station shone farther down the corridor. She raised her head to the ceiling and took a deep breath, then released it gradually as a tear slowly slid down the side of her face and down her neck. She was alone and right now she felt it.

Seeing her grandmother so helpless tore her apart. She was once so strong and now her body had betrayed her, but her eyes were still bright and alert. The once vibrant intellectual, who could argue and win any debate, was now rendered nearly speechless.

Gia closed her eyes in regret. Time had always been against her, but right now it was her enemy. She'd lost so many years not having her mother with her. There was no way she could face losing her grandmother, too. She missed so much for so long. She just wished she could have it all back. She turned, glancing back into the room. Her grandmother was sleeping peacefully, just as she had been for the past half hour. The small lamp was on and the room was set in a comfortable muted glow. Gia walked back into the bedroom and picked up her coat and purse, then paused at her grandmother's bedside. It was time for her to head home.

As Gia walked out of the room she smiled, thinking about the last time she and her grandmother had been together. It was at her condo in the city. They were cooking and eating dinner and, as usual, arguing about politics, something they did often. Her grandmother had an insatiable appetite for political science, and she was her grandmother's perfect match. She just wished they had had more time.

Gia grew up living with her paternal grandparents and father, between his many unsuccessful marriages. For years she'd been told the worst about her grandmother. It wasn't until years later that she found out that she'd been lied to all along. After that she promised herself that she'd make it up to her grandmother.

This wasn't the first time her grandmother had had medical problems, she thought as she continued walking down the empty corridor. The last time was right after grad school. Gia was working in a law office in Boston. Her grandmother had come to visit and then had a heart attack and was hospitalized a day later. The gut-wrenching sight of her grandmother so completely incapacitated tore her apart inside. At her grandmother's insistence, no one except her doctor knew what had happened. Her grandmother returned to Philadelphia, and a few months later she followed. She'd been at her grandmother's side ever since.

"Are you okay?" one of the nurses asked, looking up from the computer screen.

Gia turned and smiled. "Yes, I'm fine. Thank you for everything you've done for my grandmother. I really appreciate it," she said.

"You're very welcome and don't worry. Your grandmother will be just fine in no time at all. Her physical therapy is doing really well and she's almost one hundred percent with her speech."

Gia nodded. "Thank you."

"Would you like someone to escort you to your car?"

"No, that's okay, I'll be fine. You have a good night."

The nurse nodded and went back to what she was doing on the computer. Gia continued down the corridor to the bank of elevators. She took the elevator down to the first floor and then walked toward the front lobby. As she got close to the main exit, she saw a man sitting in the waiting area. The closer she got to the exit, the more recognizable he was. She stopped a few feet away. She was too stunned to speak. All she could do was shake her head in disbelief. Then one word tumbled from her lips. "Keith."

He looked up and then quickly stood. "Gia," he said softly.

"What in the world are you doing here?" she asked, speaking very slowly. "And don't tell me you just happened to be driving by."

"This looks wrong. I know that. And I know you're feeling exposed, but I don't—"

"Exposed, ya think?" she quickly interrupted. "I can't believe you. This, my personal life, is none of your business. It has nothing to do with you. How dare you—"

He hurried toward her. "Gia, please wait—"

"You followed me," she stated, obviously appalled by his audacity. "I can't believe this. Are you some kind of nutcase stalker or something?"

"No, no, I promise you, I'd never do anything like that ordinarily, but I was just—"

"What? What? What could you possibly say to me to make this look right? No. I don't want to hear it. I don't care what you were doing. You followed me here. That's called stalking. There are laws against stalking another person in this city. I can't believe— "

"Look," he said sharply, instantly stopping her tirade. He looked around, as did she. They were the only ones in the lobby except for a young man wearing earbuds polishing the floor with a large humming machine on the other side of the large open space.

He wasn't paying any attention to them. "Just hear me out," he said much more calmly.

"Fine, explain. What are you doing here?" Gia said hastily.

"I wasn't stalking you. I was concerned. You ended our conversation so abruptly back at the office and then you drove past me like the world was about to end. At first I just wanted to make sure you were okay. Then when you didn't immediately come back out, I thought I'd wait here for you."

"You've been waiting here all this time for me," she said.

"Yes." He nodded.

She looked at him, feeling foolish. She had over-reacted. She looked away. "Okay, fine, you were concerned. You still shouldn't have followed me. This is very private."

"Yes, you're right and I understand that. I should never have invaded your privacy like this. I'm truly sorry. But as I said, I was concerned. Is it your grandmother you're here visiting?"

Gia nodded and began walking toward the huge windows surrounding the lobby area. "Yes, she had a stroke."

He nodded. "I heard. Is she going to be okay?"

She nodded wordlessly. Saying the words was still too difficult. She felt emotions welling up inside her. She swallowed hard, trying to hold back the tears that always threatened whenever she was here. "She was getting better, but then this evening she had a fall."

"I'm sorry." He walked over and stood behind

her, but kept enough distance not to make her nervous. "How is she?"

"She'll be fine. No broken bones."

"Good," he said, then looked around the empty lobby. "I've heard of this facility. It's very well respected. I understand they do exceptional work here."

She looked up, seeing his reflection in the darkened glass. He turned, looking right at her. Piercing dark eyes met tearful ones. "Are you okay?" he asked softly.

She nodded. "Yes, I'm fine. I'm just going to sit a moment."

He nodded. "Then I guess I should go. Good night."

"Good night," she said.

He didn't move. He just stood staring at her reflection. Then a few seconds passed. "Good night," he said again, then started walking away. A few feet away he paused and looked back at her. "Have you eaten yet?" he asked.

She turned to him. "No, not really, just a couple bites of cold pizza, that's all," she said.

He walked back over casually. "I know a great place—good food, wonderful service, quiet and it's not too far from here. I was gonna stop by and grab something to eat on the way home," he said. "Would you like to join me?"

"No, thanks, that's probably not a good idea."

"Are you sure?" he asked, moving closer. "How about this? We go to the restaurant in separate cars.

We sit at two different tables with no direct contact. We can even pass notes between our waitresses."

She laughed at the image of his silly suggestion. "Thanks, I think I needed that right now, but as for your very generous and very odd invitation, not a good idea," she repeated. "Thanks anyway."

He nodded. "Okay, if you're sure. Good night." He leaned in and kissed her cheek tenderly. As he leaned back she opened her mouth and in an instant their lips almost touched. It was sweet and innocent.

Then she initiated something that shouldn't have happened. She reached up, grabbed his jacket and held tight. A split-second's pause evaporated. She kissed him, releasing more passion than even she had imagined. The instant their lips touched, there was no control, only need and desire. Keith's tongue slipped into her mouth and she opened for him, giving as much as she received.

Her heart fluttered uncontrollably as she moaned deep in her throat, yearning for still more. This kiss was everything she had imagined and more. Her body simmered as she drowned in the sensual feel of being held in his arms. She felt everything all at once, including the fact that this had to stop. When the kissed ended, she collapsed against him and he stood strong, holding her in his powerful embrace. Neither said a word. She stepped back and looked away. He then turned and left in silence as if it had never happened.

She stood watching him walk out of the building, get into his car and then drive out of the parking lot.

She waited a few minutes, thinking about what had just happened. Justifying it was easy. She was distraught and he was there. Then she went to where he'd been sitting earlier and sat down. She wasn't sure what to make of seeing him again. Following her was definitely not cool, but then he had stayed this late and waited for her out of concern. She took a deep breath, touched her lips and released the breath slowly. Keith Washington was definitely different than what she had expected.

She looked around, seeing the young man on the polishing machine still working hard. He was much closer than before. She assumed she was probably holding him up. It was late and it was time to leave. She grabbed her things and walked to her car. She got in and as soon as she inserted the key she heard her stomach growl. Not feeling like cooking when she got home, she decided to grab something on the way in. There was a little all-night diner not too far from where she lived. She went there sometimes after leaving the nursing home. The food was delicious and they were friendly and fast.

The parking lot of the small eatery was more crowded than Keith had expected. Usually he parked right in front, but tonight he had to park along the side. As soon as he walked in, he was greeted by a familiar face. "Hey, Keith, you're early tonight," the waitress said as she escorted him to his usual booth in the back.

"Hey, Gladys. Yeah, I guess I am."

"Decided to take the night off, huh?" She added, "Well, good for you. You work too hard. You need an early night sometimes."

"Nah, not quite, I'm gonna head back to the office later. So, why's it so crowded in here tonight?" he asked as he slid into his booth.

"Some cheapo decide to call this his wedding reception. Twenty-five people came in unannounced three and a half hours ago and just had to sit together. We actually asked a few customers to move and give them the entire back area. Long story short, they're noisy, belligerent and totally obnoxious to the other patrons. They ordered and ate just about everything on the menu and now they're walking out without leaving me and Lois a single penny as a tip, and this after the idiot groom tried to hit on Lois the whole time. I don't know if the bride knows it or not, but she is in for a rude awakening and one helluva cheap honeymoon."

As she spoke, her voice got louder and louder. It would have been impossible for the last few stragglers from the wedding party not to have heard her disgruntled jabs. Keith shook his head. This was his favorite place to come. The food was excellent and the people were real.

"Well, I'm sure your good service will be well rewarded."

"Yeah, well, not by them fools," she said. Lois, the other waitress, laughed as she passed by, leaving a glass of water on his table in front of him.

"So, what's tasty in the kitchen tonight?" Keith asked.

"Besides me, I'd go with the green beans, mashed potatoes, gravy and meat loaf or the collard greens, potato salad and grilled chicken. They're both excellent and Twister stuck his foot in those collard greens, metaphorically of course."

Keith chuckled. "Sounds good, I'll go with the grilled chicken, potato salad and metaphoric collard greens."

"You got it," she said, nodding, then sashayed away. Keith shook his head. He'd been coming here for years, and since he seldom cooked, this was like his second home. He picked up his glass of water, took a sip and then pulled out his cell phone. Since leaving the nursing home, he'd gotten three messages. One from Megan and the other two were messages from his brothers, Jeremy and Drew. They both texted the same message—Tomorrow!

An instant shiver shot down his back. He knew that word would come soon, and here it was. He didn't need to email them back. He knew exactly what they were talking about. His great-aunt, Louise Marie Gates, was coming tomorrow. He shook his head miserably. On top of everything else, this was the last thing he needed. Just as he deleted the two emails, his cell phone rang. It was Drew. He answered. "Yeah, I just got your email."

"Bro, I hate to have to do this to you, but…"

"Yeah, I know. I'm up," Keith said, looking up and

around the diner. He took a deep breath, realizing he had no idea how he was going to get out of this.

"She's coming in tomorrow and she needs someone to pick her up. Coincidentally, Jeremy and I are both busy."

"Doing what?" Keith asked.

"We're picking up cigars for the office."

Keith chuckled, understanding Drew's not-so-subtle reminder. He'd lost the pull and now he had to step up. "Yeah, okay."

"But you're in luck. I hear it's a short visit. Mom said she's just here for Prudence and Michael's benefit ball and then to visit an old friend, something about mediating a family drama."

"Good, hopefully that'll keep her busy. Is Colonel Wheeler coming with her?"

"I don't know. Are you gonna stop by the house tonight?"

"No, I'm at the diner right now. I'm gonna head back to the office after this. I have a few things I need to take care of. I'll go by the house tomorrow evening. In the meantime, I'll think of something."

"Okay. How did that other thing work out this evening?"

Keith smiled. His thoughts instantly went to Gia. Seeing her smile and hearing her laugh as he had joked about them creatively eating dinner together made him chuckle now. "I'm not sure yet."

"Did you meet with her?"

"Yeah, we met. I told her I'd set up something more formal in the next few days."

"It sounds tricky. Good luck on that."

Keith's second line beeped. He checked the caller ID. It was his mother. "Yeah, I have a feeling I'm gonna need it. I'll talk to you later." He clicked over. "Hello, Mother, how are you?"

"Hello, darling, I'm completely rushed. Question—how crazy busy are you after Friday's press conference? I know your father doesn't have anything planned for you. What does your schedule look like?"

Keith frowned. He had a feeling he knew exactly where she was going with this, but right now he didn't have much of a choice. "I can probably shake some time loose."

"Great, I need a favor," she said.

"Sure, what do you need?"

"Mamma Lou changed her plans. She's coming into town sooner than expected. I need you to pick her up at the train station." Keith paused, going silent. "Keith, are you still there?"

He cleared his throat. "Yeah, I'm here. Um, sure, send me the details and I'll be there."

"Good, thank you, sweetie. I'd hate to have to send a car to pick her up. You have a good night. I'll forward you the information in the morning."

"Good night." He disconnected just as his meal arrived. He looked at the succulent meal in front of him and frowned. It looked delicious, but suddenly he wasn't as hungry as he thought he was. He dug in, though. The food was delicious and once he started eating, his appetite returned.

Chapter 6

Gladys stopped by his table fifteen minutes later. "Keith, I was asked to give this to you by a young lady waiting for a takeout order. You know I'd never do this ordinarily, but she said you knew each other." She handed him a folded piece of paper.

"Really?" he said, taking the paper and unfolding it. He read the message and chuckled. *"I assure you I'm not following or stalking you. But imagine my surprise at seeing you eating at my favorite takeout diner."* He looked up and turned around and saw Gia sitting at the counter behind him. He nodded. She nodded.

"Now, if she is lying and she's some kind of crazy stalker lunatic, I'll have Twister kick her little butt out of here."

"That won't be necessary," Keith said, pulling out a pen. He began writing on the same piece of paper.

"She looks a'ight, real cute, but you know that don't mean nothing nowadays. She might be outta her ever-loving mind."

He wrote *"join me"* on the note, refolded it and then handed it back. "Gladys, would you please take this to the young lady and see if there's a reply."

"Sure," she said, looking puzzled, then walked away.

Keith smiled. This was certainly something he hadn't anticipated. He dug his fork into his collard greens and put them in his mouth. The tart-sweet-spicy-succulent taste had just enough pizzazz to excite his taste buds. Gladys was right. Twister had really outdone himself. After that he ate the potato salad and sliced some grilled chicken. Just as he wiped his mouth and was sipping his water, Gladys returned. She slid the piece of paper to him. He picked it up and read it. It continued the conversation.

"Sorry. Can't. I believe this was your suggestion. 2 cars. 2 tables. No direct contact."

He wrote his answer. *"I changed my mind. I want direct contact."* He underlined the word *direct,* then folded the paper and placed it where Gladys had put it. Lois came by a few seconds later, picked it up and kept going. He continued eating. She returned minutes later and placed the folded paper in the same spot.

He opened and read it, then laughed out loud. *"Careful what you ask for—you might just get it."*

He wrote *"I hope so. I like living dangerously. Join me."*

After a while the note passing had become a ballet of sorts with either Gladys or Lois picking up and/or delivering.

"But what fun would that be?"

"Agreed. Your favorite takeout? I've never seen you here before."

"I've seen you."

"Really? When?"

"A few times, late at night. Same booth—working or on the phone."

"You should have come over."

"Not my style."

"I guess I have to pay better attention."

"I guess so. We're running these ladies ragged."

"Trust me. They're having as much fun as we are."

"Still."

"Fine, then join me or I'll join you. We can make this work."

Gladys returned with the note. *"Are you sure?"*

He nodded and wrote a one-word reply. *"Yes."* He placed the note in the spot. Gladys took it, then returned the note a few seconds later. Keith looked up at her, questioning.

"She's gone," Gladys said. "She asked me to give this to you after she left."

Keith turned around to see the empty counter space, then glanced around, seeing only a few people in the diner. Gia was no longer there. He looked out the window. Her car was pulling off. He looked at the note and saw the last message she'd sent him. *"As much as I may be tempted, I can't do this. Maybe another time."*

"Yes, definitely," he said aloud as he tucked the note in his jacket pocket.

"Can I get you anything else?" Gladys asked, tearing his check off her pad.

"No, I'm done," Keith said. "Thanks, Gladys, and please thank Lois, as well." He wiped his mouth needlessly, paid the check and then placed two one-hundred-dollar bills for Gladys's and Lois's tip on the table where the notes had been.

He left the diner, driving in silence. For the first time in a long while he didn't want to go back to the office. But he went anyway. He opened the door and headed to his desk. Kate had left two overnight express packages and a note from Megan. Neither needed his attention this evening. He sat, opened his laptop and pulled up the file he'd been working on. Two hours later he stopped. His mind was no longer in this. He saved his file, closed the laptop and got up to leave. As soon as he turned the office lights off, his phone rang.

Gia dragged her finger across the tiny inset pad, highlighting everything she'd just written. Seeing the massive section made her cringe. In the last hour and a half she had rewritten, edited and corrected this passage fifteen times. She shook her head, bit at her lower lip and then pressed the delete key. In the blink of an eye, everything vanished.

She sighed heavily and shook her head again. She'd just wasted almost two hours writing what sounded more like country and western lyrics than a serious business proposal requesting financial and political support. She closed her laptop and then set it aside. It was useless. She wasn't getting anything done this evening. She was too distracted.

At first she told herself it was her grandmother's health, but she knew her grandmother would be fine in time. Then she convinced herself that it was the OCC. But she knew that wasn't true. She knew exactly what was distracting her, or rather *who* was distracting her—Keith Washington.

As if to clear her thoughts, she stood up, walked to the window and looked out. Living on the top floor in a high-rise condominium right off Delaware Avenue on Penn's Landing afforded her a spectacular view. To the left were the glittering shining lights of the Ben Franklin Bridge. She looked across the Delaware River to the sparkling lights of Camden, New Jersey. At night the dazzling landscape was breathtaking. She couldn't imagine living anywhere else.

Right now this was what money afforded her— the lavishness of her home. She was born into the lifestyle, and that would never change. Her family's wealth dated back five generations. It had started in the back of her great-great grandmother's laundry. The simple card games grew into the hottest nightspot in the early 1920s. By the time prohibition became law, the Duncan family added loan-sharking and bootlegging. Just like many of the megawealthy families now, the Duncans' history began steeped in the underbelly of crime, illegal speakeasies and back-alley liquor dens. They realized early that there was money to be made, and they made a lot of it.

They took advantage of weaknesses. If customers couldn't pay their debts, they signed over their homes. Soon the Duncans owned property all over the city. By the time the prohibition laws had been repealed, her family was mind-staggeringly rich.

Today the Duncans were a respected family in the City of Brotherly Love. They were law-abiding, mostly, and had prominence and power as the city's premier real estate developers. Her grandfather was a legend, and her father was living up to it by creating his own legacy. But that's where it ended.

When she turned her back on it all, they were shocked and blamed her nonconformist mother for corrupting her family responsibilities. Her father was furious. Her grandmother collapsed and her grandfather was enraged. He disowned her on the spot. But she refused to change her mind. She just hoped they would learn to accept her life as she wanted to live it.

Gia closed the drapes and turned around, knowing it was never going to be that easy. She walked back to the desk and looked down at her laptop. There was no way she was going to try to work. She grabbed her purse and pulled out a business card. She read it—Keith Washington, Attorney at Law. She grabbed her cell phone and went into her bedroom.

She climbed into bed and rested her head back against the pillows and looked around her spacious bedroom. Stylishly decorated and accented with just the right number of antiques, it was an interior designer's dream. From the outside, her life looked nearly perfect. She had a job she enjoyed, family and friends she loved, but still she knew there was something missing. But she didn't have time to think about all that right now.

She needed to get rid of this distraction so that she could focus on work again. She glanced at the bedside clock. It was late—perfect. She grabbed the phone and business card from the nightstand and started dialing. Calling and leaving him a message at his office was a great idea. That way she didn't have to actually talk to him. She nodded. It was the coward's way out, but that was okay. She didn't mind being a coward right now.

She knew there was no way he'd be in the office this late at night. She smiled, knowing exactly what she was going to say on his voice mail. The phone rang twice, then stopped. Someone answered, "Yes."

Gia froze. "Hello," he said. "All right, I know you're there. You might as well answer since I have caller ID and already know the phone number calling."

She knew he was bluffing. There was no way her phone showed anything other than two words, "private caller," as a display. "Hello," she said timidly, "Keith?"

"Yes, Gia?" he said cautiously.

"Yes," she said, "what are you doing there this late? You're not supposed to be in the office," she said accusingly.

"I'm answering the phone. But I believe the question is, why are you calling me this late?"

"Sorry, you took me off guard. I didn't expect you to be there."

"But yet you called. Who did you expect would answer?" he asked.

"Actually, I expected to just leave a voice message."

"Sounds like the coward's way out," he joked.

"I prefer to think it was being efficient. Leaving a message tonight is one less thing I have to do tomorrow," she responded.

His deep throaty chuckle seeped through her quickly. She knew he didn't really believe her, but she also knew that it didn't really matter. "Well, Ms. Duncan, now that you have me, what can I do for you?"

She took a deep breath. "I wanted to call and thank you for tonight. It was very considerate of you to be concerned about me. But I need you to know that this doesn't negate anything between the OCC and the mayor's office."

"Of course it doesn't," he said, knowing the OCC's endorsement was all but his.

"The OCC is still going to hold the mayor accountable for his actions, or in some cases inaction."

"The mayor stands by his record," Keith insisted. She didn't reply. There was a moment of silence, and then he continued softly. "You know, you're not nearly as cynical as you pretend to be."

"You don't know that. I just might be," she declared.

"True, but I doubt it."

"And you're not as charming as you think you are," she said.

"Of course I am. At least you think I am."

She laughed. "You are shameful and you really don't know me."

"You'd be surprised what I know."

"I told you earlier not to underestimate me, Keith. I suggest you take me at my word. I will do my job."

"Of that I'd expect nothing less, since I will, too."

"Good," she said, "then we understand each other."

"Yes, we do." There was another slight pause. "I'm beginning to like this between us. I look forward to our next meeting. Perhaps there is hope for us after all."

"Good night, Mr. Washington."

"Good night, Ms. Duncan."

Gia ended the call and just sat there in her bed holding the phone in her hand. She had no idea what to make of what had just happened. After a while she reached over and placed her phone on its charging pad, then turned the light out and lay back, closing her eyes. She shook her head and smiled. The man was arrogant, exasperating, incorrigible and too damn sexy for her own good. And he was right about one thing—she did find him charming. Her last thoughts before drifting off to sleep were of Keith Washington, and images of her day appeared.

She was back at the community center surrounded by the town hall audience again. Like before, Keith was right behind her. But this time he was much closer. She could feel the singeing heat of his hot breath on her neck as he spoke. She couldn't hear what he was saying, but whatever it was she was nodding in agreement. Then she felt his large hands come up around her waist and pull her possessively back, closer to his body. She inched forward, but he held her tightly, soothing her body to relax with his words.

She looked around cautiously, but no one paid them any attention. His mouth came closer as he whispered to her again. She nodded. Then he kissed her earlobe and went lower with tiny nibbles down to her neck. Her heart pounded for more. He pressed her back closer, sealing their connection. Her legs shook and her hands trembled. Someone would see them and she'd be humiliated. But he felt too good and she couldn't stop this even if she wanted to. He slowly released the buttons on her silk shirt, exposing her bra to the room.

She opened her eyes, startled, but everyone still faced forward. He released the front clasp. The full heaviness of her breasts parted the lace material. His hands came up to caress and cup her breasts. She gasped as he fondled and rolled each nipple between his finger and thumb. The tender nipples hardened to cut diamonds.

His mouth came down to her neck again. She rolled her head back, gasping for whatever air was still left in the room. She heard her own throaty moan as her body's moisture flowed between her legs. She turned her head to the side. The kiss came in a burst of light, exploding in her mouth. It deepened steadily beyond anything she had ever felt. The intensity shot down her body to buckle her knees and curl her toes. Ravenous kisses, lustful licking and sensual suckling rocked her to the core. She shivered with surging excitement as her body melted against his.

His hands continued touching, caressing and torturing her body. She felt his hard erection press against her back. The steel of his penis excited her. "This is a dream. This is a dream. This is a dream," she murmured, repeating over and over again, knowing that whatever she did and however she did it wasn't real and because of that she could make him do whatever she wanted.

She thought about his hand between her legs, and without saying a word he wrapped his arm around her waist to hold her secure while his other hand went down. She smiled, giddy with the pleasure of her power and the rapture of this burning hunger. He touched her there, brushing his fingers first against the scant curls, then her inner thigh and finally her tiny nub. Already fully engorged, the nub throbbed and ached for more. "Touch me," she whispered.

He did. Over and over again, he toyed and tantalized. Her breathing stopped, then came again in halted gasps as her body shook to his slow, steady strokes. Her knees buckled and her legs began to wobble. "More." He thrust one finger inside her. Her muscles contracted instantly. "More." He pressed two fingers in. She fell back, but he was there to catch her. The next word never crossed her lips, but the thought was still there. He gave her more. She moved frantically to the thrusting fierceness of his fingers and hands.

Throbbing, stroking, pulsating faster and faster. With his fingers inside and his thumb torturing her, she was going to implode. She rocked her hips and he pressed deeper and deeper, ravaging her to insanity. Then she came in a muffled shriek as orgasmic shock waves shot through her over and over again. Her body shuddered and quivered as the last few quakes of passion released. Then, in an instant, he faded; everything faded as sleep took her once again.

Chapter 7

Thankfully their next meeting at the mayor's Initiative Conference was very business-oriented and very public. After the dream she'd had the night before, there was no way she could handle being alone with Keith. But being in a room with three dozen civic and business leaders and a good number of community actions groups, she felt safe.

But if Keith had been really looking forward to their next meeting as he'd said, he didn't show it. He had to know OCC was on the invited list and that she'd show up. As soon as she walked in, she paused, seeing him instantly. Dark suit and tie with striped shirt and glasses. She smiled. Any other man might have looked like a nerd, but he pulled the classic look off perfectly.

She walked in with another woman, Donna Mathers, a local intimate-apparel boutique owner. This was her first time attending the conference, as well. In spiked heels and a body-fitted animal-print dress cut down to expose her full breasts, she looked more like she was going out clubbing on a Saturday night than to a business conference, but she seemed nice enough. She was older, around fifty, but gave the appearance of being much younger. They introduced themselves, traded business cards and information, then decided to partner up for the day. Gia knew the community service people, and Donna knew some of the business leaders. Neither of them admitted to knowing the politicians well.

They hung together as promised for the first fifteen minutes of the meet-and-greet, and then Donna saw someone she knew and quickly excused herself. Gia watched her go, as did a number of men standing around. She walked away slowly, exaggerating the sway of her hips, knowing the men would be watching. Gia shook her head. It always amazed her that some women needed to perform for attention.

"Hello, Gia."

She'd know that deep, sexy voice anywhere. She turned and smiled politely. "Keith, hello, how are you?"

"I'm doing great, you?"

"Good, real good,"

"So, I see you weren't too busy to attend this year."

"What do you mean?" she asked.

"Bill usually attends with your apologies. I'm glad you took the interest and came this time."

She nodded, knowing that this was the first time she'd ever seen an invitation cross her desk. Bill usually handled the mail, but since he'd been so busy with local fundraising, she'd been handling it. "Yes, I am, too. It's a pleasure being here. I'm looking forward to a very informative afternoon."

"And, of course, seeing me again," Keith half joked.

"Oh, yes, of course, seeing you again," she said, playing along.

They smiled with more behind their eyes than any casual onlooker would imagine. "I'm glad to see your sense of humor has improved."

"It comes and goes," she joked.

"I want to talk to you about something," he said, grasping her elbow and moving her to the side. "The mayor's office has commissioned a new panel to help bring the political office closer to the people represented. It's a nonprofit panel representing local business leaders, city officials and interest groups. It's called the Bridge, and its main objective is to literally bridge the gap between the office of the mayor and the needs of the people."

"Yes, I've heard of it."

"Good. I'm representing the mayor's office in officially inviting you to participate on the panel."

"I'm honored, but that would be impossible. That's a full-time position."

He nodded. "Yes, it is, and since it's generally

what your organization is supposed to do anyway, I hoped—"

"Supposed to do?" she questioned quickly.

"Bad choice of wording. Would you be interested?"

She frowned. "I can't see how that would work. Now with OCC I'm beholden to no one except my conscience and the people who need our voice."

Keith looked away, frowning. "I get the feeling from your disapproving expression that you don't buy it. You want change, but you're not willing to be a part of the solution, only to complain about the problems and deny the results. The mayor is very responsive to the people. Are you?"

"I wouldn't be so overly proud of that if I were you. The mayor has a record that's filled with flaws, holes and empty promises," she quickly added, softening her voice, as well.

"A record that has also seen new citywide health and safety initiatives implemented and a cost-of-living increase for teacher, police and firefighter salaries. A record that's lowered the crime rate and begun cleaning up the city streets, and a record, I might add, that has been impeded, stalled and blocked on all fronts by the city council and still he has succeeded."

"He could have, should have, done more in three and a half years."

"Not with an obstructive city council headed by your friend."

"What friend?"

Donna chuckled as she approached. "Seriously, listen to you two. You argue like me and my ex did years ago."

Gia and Keith turned around to see Donna standing there smiling. "Sorry about that, Donna," Gia said.

"I apologize," Keith added.

"No, don't apologize. I enjoyed it," she said, turning her full attention to Keith and even blocking Gia with her shoulder. "You're both very passionate about your beliefs. So am I. It's a good thing to be passionate. You don't see enough of it these days. Hi, my name is Donna Mathers."

"Hello, Donna, it's a pleasure meeting you. I'm Keith Washington. And please disregard my conversation with Ms. Duncan. We disagree on particulars, but fully agree on purpose."

"You're an attorney, right?"

"Yes, with the Washington and Associates Law Firm." He handed her a business card.

"Nice, thanks, I might just give you a call one evening."

"Our firm is always available to assist."

"I'm sure you are," she said seductively, "firm, that is."

"Ladies, if you'll excuse me," Keith said, nodding politely, "I believe we're about to begin."

Gia stared at Donna with her mouth slightly open. She couldn't believe she'd just said that. Apparently being blatantly obvious wasn't just for her outfit. The bold leopard-print dress should have been cougar.

"Better take notes, Gia. That's how you get what you want." As Keith walked away, Donna watched and sighed admiringly. "Damn, that is one fine brother. I would not mind doing him day in and day out all night long and then some."

Gia turned to follow Donna's gaze. Sure, it was crude and a bit over-the-top, but Gia had to admit she had the exactly same sentiments. Keith was everything any women could want in a man. No wonder he had every woman in here taking a second and third look at him. He was successful, intelligent, built and too sexy. And on top of all that, he had the swagger and confidence to know it.

"Come on, let's get a good seat right up front," Donna prompted. "I want to see everything."

"Sure, sounds good," Gia said, but she was really hoping to sit in the back and as far away from Keith as possible. After the dream she'd had last night, all she could think about was exactly what Donna had suggested.

Still, one full day of seeing Keith and ignoring the way he was making her body burn was getting to be too much. Whether he knew it or not, he was driving her crazy. At one point, while giving a brief presentation, he glanced in her direction. The look he gave her took her breath away. She nearly climaxed right then and there.

And perhaps it was just her imagination, but he seemed to be staring at her from the head table the entire time. At one point it had gotten so obvious that Donna, sitting next to her, leaned over. "Is it me or is

Keith Washington staring directly at you? How well do you know him?"

She, of course, quickly disavowed any knowledge other than their very brief encounter at the community center.

Donna's expression showed she was skeptical. "You sure you want to stick with that story?"

"It's the truth."

"Uh-huh, okay, if you say so," Donna said, smiling curiously. Moments later the program took a break. Everyone stood and walked around. Donna was the first to make a beeline straight to Keith. Gia went in the opposite direction. She grabbed a glass of water in the back of the room, then turned. Keith was directly across from her with Donna and two other women in his face.

"Gia."

She turned, hearing her name, to see a wide politician's smile. Lester Jameson walked up to her, blocking her view of Keith and his fan club. "Councilman Jameson, how are you, sir?" she said.

"Councilman, sir, what is this? Please, call me Lester."

"Yes, of course, Lester, how are you?"

"Good, good," he said, speaking entirely too loud. Those close by quickly looked over, taking notice as intended. "It's good to see you. How's my favorite community organizer?"

"I'm fine, thank you."

"And when's my endorsement coming?"

"Your endorsement?" she asked.

"Where's Bill? He usually attends these functions."

"He was unable to attend. I'm sorry, you mentioned an endorsement...."

"Yes, time is getting short and having OCC's rubber stamp would seal it for me," he said, looking around in earnest. "Ah, here he is now—someone you should see."

Gia turned and stopped cold.

"Hello, Gianna," Lawrence said.

"Hello, Granddad," she said.

"Now, isn't this nice?" Lester gushed, seeing grandfather and granddaughter staring at each other wordlessly.

Keith openly bristled as his attention was focused across the room at the two people standing and speaking way too close together. It was Gia and Jameson, and it took everything he had not to storm over and end their conversation. But the last thing he wanted to do was to openly show what had been churning inside him the past few days. Gia had been on his mind too much. Earlier he had been in a meeting and found himself totally distracted and needing to completely refocus. He even went as far as to ask a client to repeat what he'd just said.

Now he was standing here listening to these two women trying to outmaneuver each other for his attention. Neither had any hopes of getting it. Ordinarily he'd be flattered, but right now he was just annoyed. But he nodded and smiled when appropriate, giving nothing away. This was part of his job as his father's front man. No one knew that this was the last place he wanted to be.

Then he saw his chance. Lawrence Duncan came over and moments later Gia walked away and headed out into the corridor. Keith excused himself and followed. As soon as he turned the corner, he saw her standing at the window looking out. He walked up and stood beside her. "Hi."

"Hi," she responded without turning to him. They stood a few feet apart, and from a distance it would appear they were not even communicating.

"Are you okay? You look a little stressed."

She smiled weakly. "I'm fine. I just didn't expect to see my grandfather here."

Keith nodded. "Lawrence comes each year. I'm surprised Bill didn't tell you."

"Yes, so am I."

"Are you enjoying the conference?" he asked, looking ahead.

"Yes, it's very informative. I'm learning a lot about how this business works."

"That's very true. Running a city, a state and a nation is a business. And every business needs a responsive leader."

"I understand the mayor will be in attendance this afternoon."

"Yes, he's on his way. Are you sure you're up to meeting him?"

"Translation," she began slyly, "will I be asking the mayor pertinent questions like the other day?"

She turned to him. "I didn't come here to confront anyone. I came to learn. And to be perfectly clear, what happened at the community center was the truth. Your father owes this city more than the last three years. We deserve better," she said.

"The city does deserve better. In fact, they deserve the best and they have it with the current mayor. His record stands for itself on creating, implementing and promoting working education and housing programs. The mayor has had to fight the city council every step of the way. Despite mudslinging politicians, bogus lies and false accusations of fraud and corruption, he's succeeded and that's the truth."

"Whose truth, your campaign-manufactured truth? That's nowhere near axiomatic," she said heatedly.

"Axiomatic, for real, you actually talk like that?" he joked.

"What, are we trading childish insults now?" she asked.

"No, of course not. Look, I just came over to clear the air. We obviously got off on the wrong foot and I'd like to rectify that and hopefully get a better understanding of what you do. Perhaps we can open a more conducive, less antagonistic dialogue between OCC and the mayor's office."

Gia felt the patronizing sting of his words. "Mr. Washington, OCC is neither hostile nor antagonistic. We merely have justifiable grievances that need to be heard, including a comprehensive jobs program."

"Admittedly, a jobs program is more challenging

to commit to, but the mayor does have a number of very viable programs on the table. And I think—"

"On the table," she snapped quietly. "You don't get it, do you? People need jobs now, right now. They don't need a handout. They need food on the table, not proposals."

"Then tell that to the city council and your benefactor, Lester Jameson, as he spews his paranoid propaganda and blocks every program the mayor's office proposes," he snapped back.

She opened her mouth and then closed it. Her temper flared. "Lester Jameson is not and never has been our benefactor. For your information, this organization is not and never has been politically affiliated. The OCC isn't bipartisan, we are nonpartisan. We stand behind no one candidate or party. We stand with and for the people."

"When you openly stand against one, you automatically stand with the other."

"That's ridiculous. We believe in fairness in politics, and when you stand up to one, it makes that one stronger."

He chuckled. "Excuse my impertinence, but exactly how long have you been in this business? You need to grow up, wildflower."

"What? Did you just call me a wildflower? Look, Washington," she lashed out at him. "You can skip the charm and cutesy name-calling. No matter how much you want to, you can't control this election by systematically excluding half the city. And if you're implying that we're on Councilman Jameson pay-roll, then—"

"I'm an attorney. I don't imply. I state facts," Keith said.

"Then your facts are wrong and you need to—"

"So this is where you got to. Good afternoon."

Gia stopped speaking instantly, noticing Blake Washington in close distance. "Mr. Mayor, good afternoon."

"How are you? Thank you for coming today. We appreciate you taking the time for this conference."

"It's my pleasure. My name is Gia Duncan," she said.

"Of course, Gia, it's good to finally meet you. I've heard some good things about you."

"Oh," she said, looking at Keith.

"How's your grandmother doing?"

"She's doing much better. Thank you for asking."

"Marian and I were truly saddened to hear that she was still in the nursing home. Please convey our most sincere wishes for her full recovery."

"Yes, I will. Thank you."

"Now, I see you two are in bit of a heated discussion, so I'll leave you to enjoy your conversation," Blake said as he reached out his hand to shake.

Gia took his hand and was immediately drawn in for a warm hug. She went willingly, instantly feeling the warmth and friendship of Blake's words. "Thank you, sir, it was good meeting you."

Blake nodded to Keith, then walked off and was quickly engulfed by a number of local business leaders. She turned back to Keith. "He seems like a really nice guy."

"He is, but what did you expect, open hostility?"

"No, I get enough of that from you," she said jokingly. He smiled. "I guess we have got to stop doing that," she said. "I'm sorry about that, this is not the time or the place. Truce?"

He nodded. "I'm sorry, too. Agreed, truce."

"I guess we're just direct opposites, like fire and ice."

"You know what they say, opposites attract," he said.

"True, but I think we're more like magnetic forces repelling as soon as we get too close."

"We both know that's not true, don't we?"

She blushed instantly. "Keith, about what happened…"

"Nothing happened. You were in need of comfort, and I was there. That's all," he reminded her, then realized he'd been standing too close and the people around them were beginning to notice. "We'd better get back inside," he said.

"Yeah, you go in first. It'll look less questionable."

He nodded and took a step, then turned back to her. "We'll talk later. It was good seeing you again," he said.

But later never came.

Chapter 8

Thursday morning, Gia woke up much later than she'd expected. She was surprised that she'd been sleeping so well, since for weeks she hadn't been sleeping much at all. Her nights were usually fitful and restless. Most nights she just stayed awake and stared out into the night or worked until daybreak, making herself cranky and edgy the next day. But the last few nights were different. She woke up feeling refreshed and energized and charged into her day full-force.

She exercised, showered, dressed and then decided to work from home for a few hours before visiting her grandmother and then going into the office. She called in to let Bonnie know that she'd be out the entire morning. Then she grabbed a cup of tea and sat down at her desk and began to outline a workable agenda and some basic initiatives for her first meeting with the mayor.

Although she hadn't heard anything from Keith and the mayor's assistant hadn't called to set up an appointment, she trusted that he was a man of his word. They had a truce and she intended to honor it.

Of course, thinking about a meeting with the mayor immediately made her think about seeing Keith. And that reminded her of the dreams she'd been having recently. She didn't exactly remember them in detail, but she knew they were on the amorous side and had everything to do with him. She wondered what Freud would say. Probably that she was subconsciously living out some erotic fantasy and that he simply represented a much-needed physical release.

Curiously, in the guise of doing more research, she looked Keith up online again. She read through a few screens and then clicked to the images profile at the top of the page. Dozens of photos appeared. She enlarged one for a better look. The notation at the bottom stated that he was attending a political event with his family. It was a candid shot with him and his brothers. They were all handsome and smiling.

Then the next photo was at the same event, but this time he was standing with a woman. She was looking up at him as if he ruled the universe. The awestruck admiration in her eyes was amazing. She was completely mesmerized by him. Granted, he was gorgeous and he looked incredibly attractive in his tailor-made tuxedo, but that was all surface appearance.

He didn't fool her and she had no intention of playing his game and falling for his charismatic charm. Her work for OCC was too important, and too many people depended on her. Besides, she'd been through that before. Men with money and power were like little boys with toys. The more they had, the more they wanted and they didn't care how they got them or who they hurt to get them.

She thought about the conversations she'd had with him—at the community center, in her office, at the hospital and then at the conference. They were heated and passionate, but most of all they were troubling. It was obvious they didn't completely agree on politics, and the fiery passion proved it. But it was clear that they had an ongoing connection that was getting more and more difficult to ignore.

She wasn't sure what this thing going on between them was, but she was sure it was escalating. There was a spark in his eyes that she connected to. Admittedly, she liked their sparring and enjoyed their times together even when they disagreed. But it was the spark that got her. She clicked back at the photo of the woman staring up at him. There was no way she was going to be one of them—blindly staring and hoping in vain.

She'd known women like that. In college they were only there to meet a husband, preferably someone rich or with enough prospects to be wealthy. In law school they were there to meet lawyers, judges and men with power. In most cases their current marital status didn't really matter. And the men loved it. They were exactly the same—money and power. Her family's money was a major draw. Over the years, plenty of men had tried to use her. Now she was perpetually leery. Trust was almost impossible.

So of course she didn't trust Keith or his motives. He wasn't exactly the enemy or in need of money, but he was someone who might use any relationship to his advantage. She thought about the last time they'd talked. His deep masculine voice had sent a shiver through her body, and even now her stomach fluttered. He had gotten to her and she let him. "Focus," she muttered, chastising herself sternly. "Stay focused." She closed the screen and went back to writing.

For the next hour and a half she researched and came up with what she thought and hoped would convince the mayor to focus his attention on unemployment. She also suggested ideas to encourage the mayor to take a more proactive role in developing a full comprehensive jobs program focusing on lower-income families. She knew it was imperative to have everything on point and in order. The last thing she wanted to do was blow this opportunity and appear to be unprepared and wasting the mayor's time. There were a lot of people depending on her, and hopefully this was only the beginning.

After she finished, she read everything over and was pleased that her writing was more focused and definitely a lot clearer. Satisfied with what she produced, she sent out inner-office copies to Bill and Bonnie to get feedback. As soon as she pressed the send button, her cell phone rang. It was the office. She answered, "Hello."

"Hey, Gia, it's Bonnie. Are you coming in any time soon?"

Gia looked at the time on the cell phone. It was much later than she thought. "Yes, I'm gonna stop by to see my grandmother first and then I'll be in. Is everything okay there?"

"Yeah, it's all good here, at least for the moment. It's just really busy all of a sudden, that's all. No one's here except me and Linda. And the calls haven't stopped coming in. We've been on the phones all morning, plus I'm working on something for Bill. He wants me to reword the press release so we can use it when the media call for information. Linda's already put together sixteen information packages to send out. Also, I updated our website and answered online questions and checked our Facebook account. We got over fifty new friend requests overnight. I think we hit a nerve at the town hall."

Gia smiled happily. "That's great. It looks like our message is really starting to get out there. Make sure to stay on top of the social networks and keep them up to date on what we're doing."

"I will, definitely," Bonnie said.

"Anything else happening this morning?" she asked.

"Danny didn't come in. He called and said that he had to work on his blog. I think he's still upset.

He really wanted to go to the mayor's press conference today and—"

"That's not gonna happen," she interrupted.

"I know, but then when Keith Washington showed
up here Monday night, he was really pissed."

"I know, but going today is out of the question.
We've lost the element of surprise and of course, the
mayor's staff is ready for anything now. In addition,
if the mayor is willing to meet with us and talk, we
should at least give him a chance."

"I know, but Danny doesn't see it that way. Have
you read his blog lately? He's really angry. He's been
unemployed and living in a cheap hotel room for
close to two years, plus his wife left him and took
the kids. He has nothing to lose. He blames the rich
politicians and specifically the mayor."

"No, he needs to take responsibility. He chose to
quit his job as a marketing manager to stay at home
and start a blog. His wife was already unemployed.
With five kids, what did he expect they'd live on?"

"He sees Blake Washington and his family as having everything and him having nothing. He plays the
lottery and gambles constantly trying to get money.
Bottom line, he wants to be rich and get his family
back. He thinks it's all about the money."

"I can't make him rich. And if his family left him
because he didn't have money, then he had bigger
problems to begin with. There's nothing we can do.
He's already on the OCC part-time payroll."

"I know. It's just sad. People think money will

solve all their problems. But it doesn't. It only gives you more problems."

"Yeah, I know," Gia agreed. There was a second's pause as both women thought about their lives. Both came from money, but whereas Bonnie embraced her wealth, Gia rejected hers. "Any other phone calls besides the people wanting information?" she asked, hoping Keith might have called with an appointment date.

"Oh, yeah, you had a few calls from the media this morning. We had reporters from newspaper, radio and television call. Most of them were interested in an OCC sound bite. I told them to call back. They all want to set up an interview to talk to you."

"Good," she said, nodding. It was just as she'd suspected. The news media were as predictable as taxes in April. They smelled a story and wanted more. "I was hoping the town hall meeting would generate renewed interest. But okay, I'll be in in a couple of hours. Is Bill still there?"

"No, not right now, he was earlier. He said he had a few things to take care of and that he'd be back later this afternoon. I know he's got a meeting this afternoon."

"I'm on my way to the nursing home now. I'll see you in a couple of hours."

"See you later."

Gia hung up and quickly gathered her things. Ten minutes later she was headed to the garage and getting into her car. She drove to Crestar Medical Center, circling around to the rehab center in back, and found a place to park right up front. The Crestar Nursing and Rehab Center was a private facility that was reputed as the best live-in rehab center on the East Coast.

It was early so there weren't a lot of visitors yet. She signed in at the front desk and continued upstairs to her grandmother's room. She knocked, then getting no answer, walked in. "Hello, Grandmom," she said as she paused, looking around. The sitting room was empty. "Grandmom," she called out again as she walked to the bedroom and saw the bed made and everything in place. She went back to the sitting room, then, seeing the balcony doors open, walked over. She peeked out to see her grandmother sitting in a chair with the *Philadelphia Inquirer* newspaper on her lap and her cell phone at her ear. She smiled and waved her granddaughter to join her. Gia stepped out on the balcony as her grandmother ended her conversation, giving the address of the nursing center and joyfully promising to see someone very soon.

"Well, good morning, Gia," Julia Banks said.

"Hey, look at you, already up and on the phone. Good morning," she said as she leaned down and kissed her grandmother's cheek lovingly.

"Sorry about that. It was Louise Gates. She's coming into town today for a visit."

"That's great. When's she getting in?"

"She doesn't know yet, she's in Alexandria with her great-grandchildren. She'll call when her train arrives in Philly."

"Okay, let me know if she needs a ride."

"I will."

"Wow, you look fantastic," Gia said happily. "How do you feel today? How's your wrist?"

Julia nodded slowly. "I feel stiff, very sore and a whole lot silly. I can't believe I was so clumsy and fell down like that."

Gia understood her grandmother's words perfectly. The therapy was working. Her speech was still slightly slurred and her tongue was still crooked, but she was so much better than she had been weeks earlier. "The doctor said it's to be expected at times. You still don't have your full strength back yet. That stroke took a lot out of you this time. But she's encouraged that you'll be back to your old self in no time."

"I'm feeling better and stronger every day."

"That's good to hear. Are you in any pain right now?"

Julia smiled. "No, thank God."

"Good." Gia sat down next to her grandmother and touched her wrist gingerly. "This doesn't look too bad. At least you didn't break anything."

"Okay now, enough about me. Let's talk about what's going on with you. I was told you've stopped by here every night since I fell on Monday."

Gia nodded. "Yes, it's usually late and you're asleep when I get here, so I don't stay long."

"Stay long? You shouldn't be here at all. Is this what you're doing these days, hanging around a nursing home all night long? I'm sure there's something else you could be doing."

"I'm fine. I work late and came over afterward."

"Gia, working is fine. Having a career is wonderful and fulfilling, but having a life outside of that is necessary. Don't be like me. You're young, you're intelligent and you're so beautiful. You need a life. And more importantly, you need a man in your life."

Gia groaned loudly. "Grandmom, do we really have to get into all of that again? I told you a hundred times, I'm fine. I don't need a man and more drama in my life right now. Yes, maybe one day I'll find Mr. Right, but not now. No thanks."

"What you need is a man who's strong, secure and not afraid of being himself. I know he's out there, but if the only places you ever go are to the office, your condo or this rehab center, you're never going to find him. Now, there's this very attractive doctor here who—"

"No, Grandmom, please, no matchmaker, no fix-up and no blind dates," Gia said quickly, knowing exactly where this conversation was leading since this wasn't the first time her grandmother tried something like this.

"I'm just saying, a good man isn't gonna just walk up to you and say hello. You have to look for him. The alternative, of course, are the thousands of so-called men walking around here who don't have a clue what it's like to be a real man. They're afraid of everything and the only way they face their fears is to push the bravado button. Then you get married and all of a sudden everything changes. The man you married is someone else, and the fairy-tale life you thought you were gonna have is anything but."

"I'm not looking for the fairy tale."

"Just don't be like me. Don't give up on love. He's out there somewhere looking for you, too."

It was as if her grandmother hadn't heard a word she'd said about not being interested in love right now. She just kept on talking about marriage, husbands and how to avoid the bad ones. Gia stopped listening as always. She'd heard this speech a hundred times before. It was the same over and over again—don't be like me. Gia shook her head. What was wrong with being like her grandmother? She was strong, independent, intelligent and well respected. Being married could never give her what she already had.

She'd seen what love and marriage did to some women. A lot of her college friends were sinking in that boat. As soon as they said "I do" they were delegated to take a backseat in the marriage. They didn't have a voice; they didn't think and they didn't have an opinion. They just vanished. That in itself was imprisoning as far as she was concerned. Nobody should have to exist like that—nobody.

Still, Gia nodded as her grandmother continued. When she finally stopped, Gia quickly jumped in. "Grandmom, trust me, I'm fine. My life is good—no, it's better than good. So please don't worry about me. You just focus on getting well."

Julia sighed heavily. "All right, all right, I hear you," she said. "But mark my words, one of these days you're gonna hear me and know exactly what I'm talking about. Love doesn't just come around willy-nilly."

"Willy-nilly?" Gia repeated humorously.

Julia smiled. "Yes, exactly, willy-nilly."

"Okay, Grandmom, one of these days, I get it. Now, can we change the subject?" Gia said, knowing that day would never come for her. Men like the ones Julia described didn't exist anymore. Gia wasn't sure if they ever really did.

"What's this I hear about you and the mayor? I saw the news this morning," Julia began. "Mayor Washington and OCC was all over it again."

Gia smiled proudly. "The North Field Community Center town hall meeting is getting even more press than I expected. OCC sponsored it and all of the viable candidates showed up, including the mayor. We had been sending him information about our concerns on unemployment and education. He never responded, so we confronted him about his record. Three and a half years ago he ran on those issues and it's time we made him justify getting our vote when he hasn't done anything."

Julia nodded. "But he has done a lot of good for this city, Gia, as mayor, a businessman and a private citizen. You've only been back in the city for three years. You don't know—"

"Grandmom, I get that you admire him, but just because he's rich doesn't make him a saint. I'm not blinded by his family money. I mean…" she said quickly, then paused. She knew by the expression on her grandmother's face that her comment hit her hard. "What I mean is that he could have and should have been doing a lot more for this city. I just want him to step up and do what he promised."

"Gia, it's not about admiration. Blake has mobilized the city and given it a new direction. Our last mayor was an easily corrupted egocentric, and his administration fed on fear and was strife with scandal. In contrast, this administration doesn't have a scant perception of dishonesty."

Gia shook her head adamantly. This had always been a point in which she and her grandmother vehemently disagreed. "Yes, but it shouldn't be a comparison. Washington's tenure should stand on its own, not be compared to the last mayor."

"I can see you're still very passionate about this."

"I am."

"Is that all there is to this?"

"What do you mean?"

"I mean, he's a man of wealth, influence and power. He reminds me a lot of your father."

"No, no way," Gia said, knowing exactly where her grandmother was going with this. She stood and looked out over the balcony. "This has nothing to do with my father or my feelings about him and his family."

"The 'his family' is also your family."

"An accident at birth," she said quickly. "I'm nothing like them and I never will be."

"Gia, having money isn't a crime. A lot of good comes from wealth."

"I know that," Gia said, turning to lean back against the balcony.

"Do you?" Julia smiled. Gia didn't respond. "Just make sure you're doing this for the right reason. This is about the people OCC represents. It's their lives."

"I know, and I am. This city needs jobs and a better education program that works and that will help develop and sustain those jobs. They need help, and OCC is the voice they don't have."

Julia chuckled. "I bet the OCC confronting Blake at the community center didn't go over too well. I'm surprised you were able to be so successful, and I know his eldest son must have been furious."

"Keith, you know Keith?" she wondered aloud.

Julia nodded. "He's a good guy—intelligent, loyal, sweet and apparently extremely dangerous to the heart."

"What do you mean, he's a player?"

"No, at least I don't think so, not intentionally anyway. He's got his father's charm and that's like walking around with a loaded weapon. Single, straight man, attractive, intelligent and rich—he's the golden fleece of bachelorhood. I know for a fact that women go to great lengths to get noticed by him. And I know of at least a few dozen women who would drop everything and sell their mama if he would have just smiled in their direction."

Gia scoffed. "He's not all that attractive."

"And you know the media love him. As far as they're concerned, he can do no wrong. I wouldn't be surprised if he ran for office one of these days."

Gia shrugged. "If he does, then he'd better keep his campaign promises or OCC will be knocking on his door, too. Did I tell you he stopped by the office Monday night? He wants us to meet with the mayor. I'd say that's a huge step forward."

"It certainly is," Julia said, smiling.

"And we've gotten a lot more interest in OCC, too. Bill's out right now taping a segment for one of the weekend news programs. OCC is right at the front of all this. Mayor Washington is going to have to step up his program. Leadership is more than ability, it's responsibility. It's time he and other politicians step up."

Julia nodded. "I'm so proud of you," she said.

"I am my grandmother's daughter."

Julia smiled and nodded. "Yes, you certainly are. You're in charge now. You do what you have to do."

"I am. I will. And speaking of which, I'd better get to work. I have a long day ahead of me." She leaned down and kissed her grandmother's cheek. "I'll stop by later this evening."

"I'll call you tonight."

Gia nodded. "Okay." She walked to the door, sparing one last glance at her grandmother sitting on the balcony enjoying the autumn weather. She took a deep relaxing breath. Seeing her looking, talking and feeling better was a prayer come true. She needed to make sure she stayed that way.

A few minutes later she got into her car and headed to the OCC office. On the way she stopped by the local bakery and picked up donuts, Danishes and bagels before going into the office. As she walked in the office, her cell beeped. She saw that it was Bonnie calling. "Hello."

Bonnie smiled with relief at seeing her walk in. "Hey, I was just calling you," she said, hanging up. "How's your grandmom?"

"Much better, thanks. She was sitting out on the balcony reading when I got there. She looks good, almost back to her old self again."

"So she's gonna be okay, then?" Bonnie asked.

Gia nodded. "Yes. I think so. She still has a lot of therapy to complete, and she needs a lot of rest to recuperate, but the doctor and the staff are very encouraged about her progress."

"That's good. But I'm glad you came in. We might have a problem."

"Of course we do," Gia said, expecting as much as she continued to her office. "Catch me up. What's going on?" Bonnie followed closely. "And if this is about the parking problem on the side of the building, please tell the neighboring business that we are complying with the local city ordinances."

"No, it's not that, it's Danny, he's—"

As soon as Gia dropped her jacket and purse on her desk, Bill barged in, interrupting. "There you are." His dark eyes were as wide as saucers. "What the hell's going on around here? Where is everybody?"

"As I was saying—" Bonnie tried to continue.

"Bonnie, please, I'm trying to talk here," Bill interrupted.

"Have you heard anything from Washington yet? Does he want to make a deal?"

"A deal. What are you talking about? What deal? We're not making any deals with anybody."

"Yeah, right, I know. I know. Sorry, wrong word choice. I meant, what was his deal? Did you talk to him? Does he want to meet with us?"

"I don't know. I'm just getting in myself, and by the way, my grandmother's doing fine, thanks for asking."

"Gia, I'm sorry. This campaign thing is getting to me. Please tell Julia I asked about her the next time you see her."

"Um, hello," Bonnie started, waving. Bill and Gia looked at her. "Excuse me, but this is important."

"What is it, Bonnie?" Bill said sharply.

"Danny went to the mayor's press conference this afternoon."

Gia's jaw dropped as she stood. "He did what?"

"Now, that's initiative. There, see, I knew we should have gone. What happened? What did he say? Is he back here yet?"

"He didn't say a lot, but he does need someone to come down to City Hall and vouch for him."

"Vouch for him for what?" Gia asked.

"He forged press credentials and disrupted the press conference, but that's not the worst part. When security escorted him out, there was a scuffle. So now he's officially being held."

"You gotta be kidding me," Gia said.

"What the hell? Did he tell them he was with OCC?"

Bonnie shrugged. "I don't know, but he needs somebody to go down to city hall and vouch for him as soon as possible."

"I'll go," Bill said distastefully.

He headed out the door. Bonnie and Gia followed, and then Gia's cell phone rang. It was Julia. "Hi, Grandmom, can I call you back? We're right in the middle of a—"

"This won't take a minute," Julia began. "Louise is getting in earlier than she expected and she can't reach her nephew. She'll need a ride."

"Um, sure, when?"

"Right now. Her train arrives in about twenty minutes."

Gia looked at her watch. It was already early afternoon. She picked up her purse and jacket. "Okay, Grandmom, I'm on my way." It was obviously going to be one of those days already.

Chapter 9

You could barely hear the muffled echo of footsteps as hundreds of people walked the stately marble-and-slate corridors. Philadelphia's City Hall, once the tallest inhabitable building of its time and currently the seat of the city's political power, houses three branches of government. The lower levels are designated for the judicial branch and courts, the legislative houses the middle sections and the top floor is reserved for the mayor's office and the executive branch. With close to seven hundred rooms, it's still one the largest municipal buildings in the world.

Keith and Blake took the octagonal spiral granite staircase two floors down, walking the considerable distance between the mayor's office and the press room. Megan Keats walked on ahead. She got to the press room door and quietly slipped in. Keith peeked in and saw Ryan Hadley, the appointed press secretary for the city of Philadelphia, already standing at the podium. He had read the prepared statement and was taking initial questions. Keith closed the door and waited with his father for Megan to let them know when Ryan was ready.

"Ryan's still taking questions," Keith said.

Blake nodded as he continued to scan his cell phone messages. "Your mother left a text message. I'm to remind you to pick up your great-aunt Louise at the train station this afternoon."

Keith glanced at his watch. "Yes, I know. Her train arrives in two and a half hours. I have plenty of time and there shouldn't be too much traffic down Market Street this time of day."

"Just make sure you get there before she arrives. She's over eighty years old. I don't want her sitting around Thirtieth Street Station waiting alone," Blake insisted.

"I'll be there in time. There's no way I would want to be the one responsible for her being let loose on the population of Philadelphia."

"What do you mean?" Blake asked, turning his cell phone off and handing it to Keith.

"Mamma Lou and her matchmaking," Keith said, putting his father's cell phone in his jacket pocket. "If I'm late, half the city will be matched up."

Blake chuckled, shaking his head. "Aunt Louise isn't that bad," he said, looking at Keith. Keith gave him a knowing expression. Blake chuckled again.

"Okay, okay. Maybe she is, but you have to admit, her matches are very nicely done. Your cousins Tony and Raymond are deliriously happy."

"True, but I'm definitely not aiming to be her next target."

"Target? What makes you think you're a target?" Blake asked.

"I'm single. Enough said," he said simply.

Blake chuckled once more. "You've got a point there. But I don't think you have too much to be concerned about this time. It's just a short visit. She's here to attend your sister's benefit ball Saturday night and then she's headed back to Crescent Island."

"I think I'll keep out of her way just in case."

"What about the pact with your brothers?"

"What pact?" Keith asked.

"Cigars in the conference room at dawn. I believe you were left with the short one."

Keith smiled, shaking his head. He and his brothers were never able to get anything past their father. Somehow he always knew exactly what they were up to, although this time Keith had no idea how he had found out. "Yes, I'm supposed to be running interference, but that's not to say that I'll be stepping into the line of fire. No target, remember?"

Blake nodded. "Right, no target." He knew well enough that the target Keith was so leery of getting was already there. But he went along with his son's illusion. "Of course not," Blake said.

Megan stepped out into the hall. "Two minutes," she whispered.

Both Blake and Keith nodded. "But right now we need to get this press conference over with. Are you ready?"

Blake nodded. "Yes, let's do this."

Megan stepped back out into the hall and nodded for Blake to enter. Ryan announced him to the customary warm applause. Blake walked into the crowded room, then stepped up to the podium. Keith followed, standing just inside the doorway. He eyed the members of the press to gauge their expressions of interest. For the most part they focused on every word his father spoke. Some nodded and others gestured or made near-silent comments to their cameramen.

The agenda was set—employment and education were the day's main focus. The mayor would update the partnerships with a number of big businesses. Their goal was to expand and develop education and workforce training with a focus on luring more businesses to the area.

Dozens of media professionals from newspaper, radio, television and online venues attended. Blake greeted the media and began with a few brief opening statements. He announced a new appointment to his staff and then reiterated his commitment to employment and education. Afterward he opened the room up to questions.

One by one they stood in turn, announced their represented media, then asked a question of the mayor. Ten minutes in, everything was going as expected. Blake stood at the podium with Keith on one side and his press secretary, Megan, on the other. He was asked a number of difficult questions and he answered with forthright honesty. He was compassionate and understanding of his city's plight and appeared to earnestly want to make things better.

All the while, one man, seething with contempt, listened in the rear of the room. The man stood and asked a question. Midway through the answer the heckling began. Soon after, he erupted with a barrage of angry insults and accusations as his personal vendetta to upstage the mayor quickly took center stage. He was loud and intrusive, refusing to sit down or give anyone else a chance to speak. Soon, all focus turned to him and he loved it.

Blake answered his first two questions, giving him some latitude, but after a while no matter who raised their hand and who the mayor called on, he continued to bulldoze and demand answers to his questions. It had quickly gotten beyond the point of ridiculous. Soon, by all accounts, what was supposed to be a standard press conference had turned into a three-ring circus, complete with ringmaster and cast of clowns. The press conference had officially been hijacked.

"No, don't listen to him! He's lying to us. They all lie—that's what they do. They're all criminals and thieves. They take our money, our homes and our families. He doesn't care about this city. All he cares about is taking our money!"

Someone asked what media outlet he represented. When he answered that he was a blogger, security immediately moved in and escorted him out. There was a scuffle as he was ejected. Shortly afterward the press conference was cut short. Blake thanked the media for their patience and understanding. They applauded as he nodded, waved and walked out. As everyone filed out of the press room, the media immediately surrounded and began asking questions of the man who identified himself as also being a member of OCC.

"He's a liar!"

Blake stopped and turned around, looking to the end of the hall. The same man who had disrupted and been ejected from the press conference earlier had waited in the hall to continue voicing his venomous opinions. He was yelling and screaming at the top of his lungs as the news media surrounded and bombarded him with questions.

"You're a liar, Blake! Help the people you promised to help! Get my family back."

Keith seethed as he followed his father down the hall and back upstairs to his office. Neither man spoke, but as soon as the office door closed, Keith began. "That's it. First Monday evening and now today. Enough is enough. OCC has gone too far."

"We'll deal with it."

"Did you see the media outlets surrounding that guy?"

"They'll soon find he's got no substance."

"Yes, but when did that ever stop the media from focusing on them? This is the kind of thing that destroys political futures. One loudmouth stands up and after a while every nut job is gonna think it's okay. It's not."

"We'll tighten security."

"I already did. The problem is OCC. They're officially out of control."

"Keith, calm down. It's not worth getting all worked up," Blake said calmly. "We can handle this."

"That's just it, we shouldn't have to," Keith said angrily as he paced the room. "It looks like every time you open your mouth in public we're gonna have to deal with some crazy from OCC jumping down your throat. They're a bunch of loose cannons going off over there."

"All's fair in love and politics."

Keith glared as he watched the replay feedback. Megan had taped the press conference and immediately forwarded the feed to Keith. He watched on his computer pad. "I offered her an olive branch, a truce, and she does this. No, not this time. All bets are off. If she wants a war, she's got one."

"Keith, calm down. This isn't a war and it's not about getting even. The OCC is simply trying to assert their constitutional rights—freedom of speech. There's no harm in questioning someone running for public office. It's the American way. Our friend just needs to choose a more appropriate venue."

"After my conversations with Gia, I was under the impression that we had come to an understanding. I suggested setting up a meeting with you. I assumed that meant she could call off her hounds. Apparently I didn't make myself clear enough. I guess I have to be a bit clearer or more convincing," he said, finally standing still from pacing.

"Convincing," Blake repeated as he checked his phone messages.

"Leave it to me, Dad. I'll take care of OCC. I'm heading back to the office now. Do you need anything?"

"Yeah, check your cell phone."

Just then, Keith's cell phone beeped with a text message. He opened and looked at the small screen. It was an urgent message from Marion Washington—Mamma Lou took an earlier train and will be arriving in twenty minutes.

"Mamma Lou's early," Keith said, looking at his watch as he headed to the door. "I have to go. I'll see you at the house this evening. And don't worry about OCC. I'll take care of them and get their endorsement. I'll have my cell phone, of course, if anything else comes up."

The drive from City Hall to Thirtieth Street Station was a straight line west down Market Street. With traffic lights, Keith, in his Mercedes-Benz sedan, got there in less than fifteen minutes. Now the hard part would be finding a place to park. He knew midafternoon it would be nearly impossible. But then he lucked out, finding a spot right out front. He parked his car and hurried to the main entrance. He walked to the center of the cavernous station and checked the display. The northbound train from Richmond, Virginia, was due to arrive in less than five minutes. He took a deep breath, steeling himself for the inevitable.

Louise Gates was formidable, to say the least. She was over eighty years old but looked more like she was in her early seventies. She was spry and active with a determined get-up-and-go demeanor that constantly belied her years. She was often taken for granted, and that was a mistake Keith had no intention of making. She was his grandmother's older sister. When she died, Louise had stepped into the role as substitute. No one could deny that she loved and adored her family.

She was kindhearted, generous and caring. Her one flaw was her annoying habit of playing matchmaker. Sure, she had matched both his cousins Tony and Raymond with incredible women, but he was sure she'd just gotten lucky. He needed her to understand that he had no intention of getting married, so she needn't bother looking for anyone for him.

The announcement was made. The northbound train from Richmond, Virginia, was arriving at the station on track six. Keith walked over to the numbered platform stairway, joining a gathering of others also waiting for their loved ones to arrive. As soon as he got there, the escalator began to move and his cell phone beeped. He pulled it out and saw that it was his brother texting him.

Jeremy: Hey, where are you? I thought we were meeting back here at the office after the press conference.

Keith: Had to make a detour to the train station.

Jeremy: Train station? You mean...

Keith: Yep, the train just arrived.

Jeremy: Do you have a plan?

Keith: Sure. Keep my distance.

Jeremy: LOL!

Keith: Gotta go, the train's here.

Jeremy: Good luck...

Keith chuckled and nodded his response just before tucking the phone back into his jacket pocket. A second later they arrived. Just a few passengers at first; then the few soon became a mass exodus. Friends called to one another, and family hugged and kissed their relations. All the time, Keith waited patiently. Shortly the mass of departing passengers trickled to just a few. Soon he was the only person standing waiting. The escalator stopped.

He waited another minute or two, then turned to the information board in the center of the cavernous station. The train's number had been removed from the board, giving way to the next arriving train from New York. A few seconds later he saw a conductor walking up the platform steps. "Excuse me, question."

"Yes, sir, how can I help you?"

"Are there any remaining passengers from the northbound train from Richmond, Virginia?"

"No, the platform's empty. Are you looking for someone?"

"Yes, an elderly woman in her eighties, gray hair, slight build, very friendly, probably carrying a few bags. She would have gotten on the train in Richmond and gotten off here."

"Nope, sorry, I was the conductor on that run. I didn't have any passengers fitting that description. Are you sure she was taking this train out of Richmond? You know, there was also an Acela Express that got in about forty minutes ago."

"No, I'm sure. She gave this time of arrival."

"Well, she might have just missed the train or maybe someone else picked her up."

"I don't think so. Is there a paging system here?"

"Yeah, there is. I'm on my way to the main office now. What's the passenger's name?"

"Louise Gates."

"Louise Gates," the conductor repeated, "got it. I'll have her meet you here," he said, then turned to leave.

"Thanks," Keith said as he pulled out his cell phone to check messages. Since leaving City Hall he'd already gotten ten, most from news organizations requesting a comment. He scrolled down, finding the last message from his mother, then looked at the time. It was the right time and right train number, but no Mamma Lou. He was just about to follow the conductor to the office when a woman quickly rushed past him entirely focused on catching up with the same conductor he'd spoken with a few minutes ago. Only a few feet away, he overheard their conversation.

"Hello, excuse me," she began breathlessly. "Hi, do you know which platform was used for the northbound train coming from Alexandria? I'm running late and I missed the announcement."

"Yeah, it came in on platform number six. But if you're looking for someone, there's no one down there. I was the last one up."

She sighed, then looked around quickly. "Okay, is there a PA system or some way I can page someone? I'm looking for an elderly woman. She was supposed to come in on that train and I don't see her waiting."

The conductor smiled broadly, looked at her and then at Keith over her right shoulder. "Hey, you two know each other? Maybe you're looking for the same person?"

"No, I doubt it, but if you could…" Gia began, then turned, stunned, to see Keith standing right behind her. She'd walked right by him and hadn't realized it. The instant she saw him she remembered her dreams in vivid detail. Reality hit and her stomach dropped and she froze in place.

"Hello," he said. His deep voice trembled right through her.

"Keith, what are you doing here?" she asked, obviously stunned to see him.

"What are you doing here?" Keith asked, equally surprised.

"I'm picking someone up from Alexandria," she said.

"Yeah, me, too, from Richmond, but I guess I missed her."

"Her," she repeated, then immediately regretted

it. The slight smirk on his face told her he knew exactly what she thought.

"Yes, *her,*" he emphasized, more closely gauging her reaction.

"Well, I'm sure she's waiting for you somewhere around here."

"I hope so."

They stared at each other a few seconds, and then Gia turned away and looked around the large open area. "So, I guess I'll expect a phone call from you regarding our appointment with the mayor."

"I understood we had a truce."

"We do," she said.

"Ah, so I guess that would explain a member of your staff having to be forcibly removed from the mayor's press conference this afternoon. I expected civility from you," he said, the curt tightness in his voice obvious.

She grimaced. "What do you mean? I don't understand."

"Are you going to play the innocent?"

"I have no idea what you're talking about."

"I'm talking about OCC forging press credentials, slipping in and hijacking a city press conference this afternoon. I'm talking about a man screaming and yelling down the corridors of City Hall. I'm talking about how I was under the impression we had an understanding, Gia."

Her faked innocence didn't work. Of course she knew what he was talking about. As soon as she saw Keith she knew this conversation was going to happen. She also knew that she had two options, apologize for Danny's behavior or just ride through. She chose the latter. "OCC was not officially there today and I have no control of what my volunteers or employees do on their own time."

"Then perhaps you're not suited to run OCC," he said abruptly.

"I beg your pardon," she said, immediately taking offense.

"My employees do not commandeer my practice and my name and run stampeding over the city officials. And since I was under the impression that we had come to an equitable solution by my agreeing to facilitate a meeting with you and the mayor, I was—"

"A meeting is not a resolved solution, and agreeing to meet is not an ironclad understanding to suspend justified opinions. The mayor is wrong and OCC is still free to speak out at any time and any place. You have heard of the First Amendment."

"Sure, freedom of speech, but perhaps you should read the rest of the Constitution more closely. It does not include defamation of character and inflammatory rhetoric in public venues. OCC was not invited. The city's on-site press conferences are for credentialed members of the press only, not lunatics off the street with an axe to grind and the backing of what has obviously now become a radical political group."

"OCC is a community organization. Now, you may not agree with our ideology, but we have every right to represent the people and speak out on their behalf. You need to get over yourself. This isn't personal."

"Yeah, you keep right on believing that."

"And for the record, I did not sanction what Danny did. We were not supposed to be there today."

"Like Monday," he commented.

"Monday was different."

"All of it?" he questioned with interest.

She knew what he was asking. She took a step back, suddenly feeling the closeness of their bodies. "Again, I have no idea what you're talking about."

"Do you spend all of your time in denial or just some of it?"

Gia breathed in and opened her mouth to respond, then closed it quickly. She paused a few seconds. "Look, I'm not about to stand in the middle of a train station and justify my organization to you or anyone else. And whatever you think is happening here is clearly solely in your imagination. It's obvious that you'll say whatever it takes to get what you want."

"You have no idea what I want," he said.

"I can only imagine."

"Solely in my imagination, huh?" he said.

"Yes, solely *your* imagination," she said tightly.

He turned to walk away and then, in a moment, turned back, grabbed her in his arms and leaned in close. "Well, imagine this," he whispered. She gasped. An instant later he kissed her with enough combustible passion to rival the sun's energy. In the fraction of a second it took for their lips to touch, her world imploded. Everything she knew or thought she knew about a kiss, she didn't. Life was brand-new and this kiss was the beginning of everything.

For all intensive purposes pleasure had a new name and it was Keith Washington. Being kissed by him was like the big bang happening all over again. Every nucleus in every atom in her body felt as if it had been jump-started. Reality stopped being real and all of her fantasies combined into one kiss, one man.

"Well, I guess I was right. You two do know each other."

Chapter 10

The kiss ended with an abrupt breathless jolt. Both Keith and Gia turned to see that the conductor had returned carrying two large bags with Louise Gates at his side. "Yes, indeed, they certainly seem to, don't they?" Louise said, nodding happily.

"Mrs. Gates, hi, hi," Gia said quickly, nervously, hugging the older woman warmly. "How are you? You look great," she rambled.

"Oh my, Gia, look at you. You're all grown up and you're so beautiful. I bet you have men falling all over you."

Gia glanced at Keith. A nerve in his neck flinched. She didn't even want to think what that was about. She was already knee-deep in what she knew was going to be an impossible explanation. "Thank you,

Mrs. Gates. I'm sorry I arrived late to pick you up. Parking is crazy around here."

"You're not late at all, dear. I'm early. I caught one of those new faster-than-the-speed-of-light trains. It left the same time as the other train but got me here in nearly half the time. It's amazing and so comfortable. But thank you so much for coming to my rescue. I'm sorry I had to call you, but your grandmother's phone number was the last number I dialed and the only phone number I could find on that crazy cell phone of mine. I don't think I'll ever be able to work that thing properly."

"That's quite all right, Mrs. Gates."

"Oh dear, please call me Mamma Lou. Everyone else does. And I see you've met my favorite nephew, Keith," she added.

"Um, nephew," Gia began, almost speechless.

Keith quickly stepped up. "Hello, Mamma Lou. It's good seeing you," he said smoothly as he leaned down and kissed her cheek.

She held, then tapped the side of his face, smiling. "Keith, you are just as handsome as your father. Thank you for coming, as well. I know how busy you are with the election and all."

"Ah, that's where I've seen you before," the conductor said, still holding the bags and standing at Louise's side. "You're Blake Washington's son. Yeah, that's right. I knew I recognized you from somewhere—the news, right?"

"Why don't I take these from you? I'm sure you have to get back to work," Keith said while slipping the man a very hefty tip. "Thank you, I appreciate your help in finding my aunt."

"No problem. No problem." The conductor nodded and relinquished the bags. "You're welcome, anytime." He glanced at the folded bill in his hand and smiled broadly. "Wow, thanks, Mr. Washington. Tell your father I'm with him all the way. He's the best mayor we've had in the city in years."

"Thanks, I'll pass that on and thanks again for your help."

"I'm just doing my job. I'm glad you all found each other."

"Yes, indeed, I'd say they certainly have," Louise said softly.

"Mamma Lou, no, it's not what you think. What you saw wasn't what you saw." He kissed her cheek in welcome. "Gia and I were just talking and—"

"Talking?" Louise said questioningly.

"Yes, talking," Gia said, quickly chiming in, "that's right. It's really not what it looks like or what you think. We were just talking about imagination and then we—"

"Imagination," Louise repeated.

"We kissed. Actually, I kissed Gia. She had no idea—"

"It was a joke, we were just playing around," Gia continued.

"Yes, exactly, that's right, we were playing around."

"It was just a kiss. No big deal. It didn't mean anything," Gia added, looking at Keith. He turned to her. His eyes narrowed. Without a single word he stole her breath away.

"Of course not," Louise said happily.

Keith groaned inwardly. It was obvious she'd not only seen the kiss, but also heard the last part of their discussion. After that they went silent. The quiet only lasted a few seconds, but to Keith and Gia, it lasted a few hours. Louise stood watching. That tiny spark of attraction she had hoped to see in them was more like a lightning bolt streaking across the sky.

"Um, I need to get back to work," Gia said.

"Of course, dear, and thank you again. Please tell your grandmother that I'll stop by the nursing home first thing in the morning."

"I will," Gia said, backing up. She never took her eyes from Louise. There was no way she could chance looking at Keith right now. "Okay, I'll see you later." She turned and hurried off.

"Well, I guess we'd better be on our way, too," Louise said.

"Yes, this way," Keith said. They walked in the opposite direction from where Gia went. Louise began talking about the people in the main office and how kind they were to her. Keith listened, then turned around. As soon as he did he saw Gia walking past the Angle of Mercy statue. She turned. For an instant their eyes met across the cavernous space. Then just like that she was gone. Keith turned and kept walking.

"Gia is a lovely woman, don't you think?"

"I wouldn't know. I don't know her that well."

"You seemed to know her well enough earlier."

"Mamma Lou…" Keith began in warning as he shifted both pieces of luggage to one side and tilted his elbow down to her.

Louise tucked her arm in his lowered elbow. "I know. You were just talking about having an imagination."

He nodded. "Yes, something like that."

Keith knew how transparently lame that excuse sounded, but neither of them was prepared to explain what had just happened. Hell, he had no idea what happened and he initiated it. He kissed her. It was impulsive and reckless. If he wanted to end the conversation, there were plenty of ways to do it. Kissing her should have been last on his list.

But the truth was she'd been on his mind way too much and seeing her again prompted him to wonder what tasting her again would be like. He licked his lips as if to refresh his memory once more. But he needn't bother. He already knew. She tasted like pure heaven.

"You know, I've known Gia Duncan since she was two days old. Her mother, rest her soul, was a good friend and when she died I watched out and kept an eye on her and her grandmother. Gia turned out so wonderfully. Her mother would have been so proud of her. But I knew even then that she'd be special. She's kindhearted and just as sweet as a summer peach, just the type of woman any man would want to have by his side."

Keith knew this slow stroll down memory lane

was going someplace, and as usual for Louise Gates it was headed straight down the aisle to the altar. "Mamma Lou, please no matchmaking this time. I am not currently and will not in the near or distant future be ready to settle down and marry. So you're wasting your time playing matchmaker with me."

"Matchmaking, Keith Washington, I don't know where you get these ideas. Who said anything about me matchmaking?" she said. "I have no idea where you got that idea. I merely mentioned that Gia was a wonderful woman."

"Yes, I'm sure she is, but I'm not interested."

"Of course not, I have someone else entirely in mind for Gia."

"Who?" he asked way too quickly.

"You don't know him. But trust me, he's absolutely perfect for her. He's tall, handsome, intelligent, charming with a generous spirit and that's exactly what she needs in her life. She's had some hard times in the love department. She needs someone to love and cherish her, and this man will."

Their conversation suddenly lapsed into silence as they walked side by side out the Market street door to his car. Keith dropped the luggage at the rear of his car and escorted Louise to the front passenger door. He opened it and helped her inside, then secured her seat belt for her. He closed the door and popped the trunk. As he placed the two pieces of luggage inside, he thought about the man Mamma Lou had chosen for Gia. He instantly took a dislike of this *him*. Whoever he was, he certainly wasn't good enough. He slammed the trunk's hood much harder than he expected. As soon as he got in the car, Louise smiled at him. "Are you all right, dear?"

"Yes. Fine," he said curtly as he started the engine and pulled away from the curb. The car behind him blew his horn, but Keith kept right on driving.

Louise translated his abrupt comment with ease. As soon as she saw his face, she knew she had to do it. The remark that she was only there to match Gia with another man got to him. It was the icing on the cake since he'd been tense and slightly off ever since Gia walked away. "Did I mention that I made a quick stop in Alexandria to see Tony, Madison and my great-grandchildren? I realized that I hadn't seen Jonathan and Johanna in months. They are so adorable. At three years old they're all over the place. They're laughing, talking, running, jumping and it was pure chaos. I loved every bit of it. So, tell me, how did the press conference go this afternoon?"

"It didn't go as well as expected."

"That is unfortunate. Is there anything I can do?"

"No, I'm afraid not. I need to do some damage control this afternoon. My team has already started."

"I still have quite a few very influential friends here in the city. I'd be happy to make a few phone calls."

"No, we'll be fine. I just have a few things to take care of."

"Well, then, you'd better get to them. Instead of taking me to the house, you can drop me off at City Hall."

"Dad's in meetings the rest of the day."

"No problem, it's been years since I've seen Marian on the bench. I always loved watching her work."

"Are you sure?"

"Absolutely," she said.

"I don't know what her afternoon schedule is like, but I know she'd love to see you," Keith said as he pressed a button on his steering wheel. "Call Mother, office," he announced. The car's phone system immediately began dialing. In a few seconds he was connected. Marian Washington's assistant answered her phone. "Janice, it's Keith. Is my mother in court this afternoon?"

"Yes, although there should be a break coming up soon. Can I give her a message for you?"

"Actually, a family member would like to sit in on proceedings. Is that going to be a problem?"

"No, not at all. I can meet you in the garage and escort them to chambers."

"That would be great. I'm on my way to City Hall right now. I'll be there in about five minutes."

"Okay, see you in a few."

Keith disconnected the call. "Okay, you're all set. Are you sure you want to spend the afternoon in court? I can always take you to the house to relax after traveling all morning."

"Oh, heavens no, I've been relaxing for the last seventy years. I'll be fine. You have work to do, and I have work to do, as well."

"You do? What kind of work?" he asked.

"Matchmaking Gia, of course," she said.

Keith frowned. That wasn't exactly what he wanted to hear. "Yeah, of course," he grumbled openly as he circled City Hall and pulled into the underground parking area. Janice was standing at the security check-in entrance as soon as Keith's car pulled up. He parked to the side and got out to open the passenger-side door. Louise got out and Keith introduced her to Janice, who had already begun the security process.

After a few pleasantries, Janice helped Louise sign in and receive her visitor's pass. Moments later she was all set. "Well, goodbye, dear. I'll see you this evening," Louise said.

"Yes, I'll see you at the house tonight, Mamma Lou," Keith said, then kissed her cheek and got back in his car.

Louise watched Keith's car drive away and mingle in with the traffic circling City Hall. In a few moments he was gone. She turned to Janice and they continued the conversation they'd started while heading to the elevators. As Janice talked about the history and architecture of the building, Louise mulled over her course of action. It was sneaky. It was devious. But it was brilliant as usual.

She smiled to herself, pleased with her latest stroke of genius. The evidence was as clear as could be. And if the kiss she'd witnessed at the train station was any indication of what was to come, this match was going to blow the others right out of the water in no time. She knew they would be a perfect match. Two not-so-willing open hearts, both waiting to be connected, even if they didn't know it yet. How perfect would that be?

She shook her head in exasperation. She had no idea why people challenged and fought against her so hard. In the end she was always right. It was like this most of the time, although she could never see the problem. She was performing a service. In days past, families would line up to visit a matchmaker. Numerous cultures praised and revered matchmakers and marriage brokers.

And now it was the same service the online dating sites performed, but she was much more accurate and thorough. She always knew the two people and she always gave them the opportunity to refuse if there was no spark. But as always she knew there would be a spark. There was with her two sons, with her two grandsons and of course the several dozens of other matches she'd successfully made.

She thought about seeing the moment Keith and Gia had spotted each other. Then of course there was the kiss. Yes, there was most definitely a spark. Her job was to keep it ignited while nature ran its course. Other than that she didn't interfere—much.

Keith headed straight to the office. By the time he sat down at his desk, everything he needed was waiting for him. Megan did a full bio on the press conference crasher. He wasn't much more than expected. Out of work, living on the edge and blaming everyone for his drama. He read her report, then strategized an appropriate solution.

The distraction of fixing the afternoon's press conference was exactly what he needed. By the early news hour, most of the local media were all over the story. They called it the City Hall press conference crasher incident. Some, of course, pointed a finger at the mayor, but they were going do that anyway. It was their process. Whatever happened, no matter what it was—blame the mayor and his leadership team.

But by the second hour, the media had soon changed their tune, leaving his father's opponents and adversaries to scramble quickly to not appear to be fools. As expected and planned, his actions were seen as disrespectful and scornful. With Keith's help the irate press conference crasher had become a security risk with questionable restrain. Keith planted the seed with questioning what the man might consider doing next, and the media ran with it. By the next half hour's news, most media outcasts questioned his motives and backing.

It was brilliant.

By seven o'clock Keith was confident that he had a handle on the flow of information again. He'd gotten approving and congratulatory messages from his father, his brothers and other associates. He sat back with Megan's repost and prepared for the next crisis. He knew this man, and this issue wasn't going away. Ultimately he'd have to finish it. And there was only one way to do that—make OCC completely irrelevant or go away permanently. Thus far he hadn't decided which.

He reached over and grabbed his desk phone. "Kate, I need you to set up an appointment with OCC."

"Sure, when do you want it?" she asked.

"Make it as soon as possible."

"Okay, before or after your trip to D.C. next week?"

"Make it after and make it here in this office."

"Okay, I'll set it up."

"Thanks," he said, then hung up the receiver.

Five minutes later there was a knock on the door. He looked up just as it opened. Kate walked in with two express mail packages. "These just came, both from D.C." She placed them on his desk and then picked up a package that had already been sealed and was ready to be picked up. She looked at the address and nodded. "Anything else to go out tonight?" she asked.

"No, that's it, thanks."

Kate nodded. "Okay, I'm headed out. I assume you're working late. Do you want me to order takeout dinner in for you—Japanese, Chinese or the usual, something from the diner?"

"Not tonight, I'm having dinner with the family," he said, then glanced at his watch. "As a matter of fact, I've got to get out of here in a few."

"Okay, see you tomorrow. Oh, yeah, I juggled a few things on your schedule. Next week your Tuesday afternoon meeting in New York is now a teleconference call. You need to be in D.C. Wednesday all day and you have a meeting here in your office with OCC Friday afternoon at three."

"Perfect. Thanks, Kate. Have a good evening."

"You, too, good night," she said, waving as she turned and walked out the door, closing it behind her.

Keith took a deep breath and leaned back in his chair, stretching. Then he opened his computer schedule to see OCC already added. He smiled. Seeing Gia would definitely be a welcomed sight. He reached up and touched his lips while shaking his head. Kissing her in public probably wasn't one of his better ideas, but it sure as hell felt good. Her lips were soft and tender and tasted like sweet honey. He certainly wouldn't mind tasting her again, but he seriously knew he didn't have a chance. Seeing her expression said it all. She was stunned after their lips parted. But he had a feeling it was more because of her own very willing reaction than the kiss itself.

A few minutes later there was another knock and the door opened. Jeremy walked in. "Hey, don't forget we have dinner at the house. You headed out soon?"

Keith looked at his watch. "Yeah, I'm right behind you."

"Okay, see you there." Jeremy left.

He stood, preparing to leave for the day. Just as he packed and closed his briefcase, his cell phone rang. He recognized the number. He read the text message and responded.

Gia: We need to talk.

Keith: I agree. The appointment is scheduled for next Friday.

Gia: No, sooner, it's personal, not professional.

Keith: Your place of mine?

Gia: Neither.

Keith: Your office?

Gia: No. Yours?

Keith: Fine. When?

Gia: Is twenty minutes okay?

Keith: I'll be waiting.

Gia: Thanks.

Keith ended the call, then sat back down and opened his briefcase again. He smiled to himself as he dialed his brother and left a text message. I'm gonna be late. Start without me.

He didn't wait for a response. He closed his cell and took out the two sealed express packages and opened one. He pulled out the contents and began reading through, expecting the after-hours buzzer to ring momentarily. It didn't. After the first half hour he made a few phone calls and prepped a few documents for review, then glanced at his watch. It had been over an hour since Gia texted him. Busying himself, he waited another half hour, then decided to leave. Apparently he was mistaken. He wasn't going to be late to the family dinner after all.

He grabbed his jacket and cell phone off the desk, then headed for the outer office. He was the last one out, so he set the alarm and locked the front door. As soon as he got to the elevators, he remembered what Mamma Lou had said. She was here to match

Gia with who she thought was perfect for her. A cold chill shot down his back.

He'd never been blown off before. He was not in a good mood.

Chapter 11

After the craziness at the train station, Gia wasn't ready to go back to the office just yet. She needed to think, and she knew the perfect place. She drove down Market Street and made a left toward Ben Franklin Parkway. It was four-thirty Friday afternoon and traffic was already horrendous. She made her way down the Parkway to circle onto Kelly Drive. She drove up behind the Philadelphia Museum of Art and parked. As she turned off the ignition, her cell phone rang. She checked the caller ID and saw it was her friend Val Emery. Relieved, she answered while getting out of the car. "Hey, Val, perfect timing."

"Hey, girl, what's up? I just called your office. Bonnie told me you were running an errand for your grandmother in the city. Where are you? Do you want to do a late lunch or early dinner?"

Gia walked over to look out at the Schuylkill River. The college crew boats were already on the water. "I'm not hungry, how about a raincheck on dinner. I'm at the Art Museum."

"Sure, no problem. Wait, you're at the museum. Uh-oh, that means trouble. The only time you go there is when something happened. What's wrong and do you need me to file papers?"

Gia smiled. She'd known Val for years. They'd attended law school together and bonded instantly since both were originally from Philadelphia. "Nah, no papers this time. You'd probably lose."

"Me, lose a court case, hardly. Who's the problem?"

"Keith Washington."

Val laughed. "Keith, are you kidding? He's a sweetheart. Wait, does this have something to do with what happened the other day at the community center?"

"That's where it started, but it's getting complicated."

"What do you mean complicated?"

Gia paused, considering how much she was going to tell her friend. It was obvious that she knew Keith. She just had no idea how or for how long. "We're not exactly seeing eye to eye on a few issues, and when that happens it gets very complicated."

"Of course you're not seeing eye to eye. His father is running for mayor and you work as a community organizer. The two of you butting heads is mandatory."

"It's not just the butting heads part," Gia confessed.

"What else?"

Gia took a deep breath. "He kissed me."

"Oh."

"Actually, that's not quite all of it. I kissed him first—Monday at my grandmother's nursing home. He kissed me at the train station this afternoon." There was a very definite pause. "Val, are you there? Is that all you have to say?"

"Yeah, I'm here, so did you kiss him back?"

"Yes," Gia said, breathing out the word slowly.

Val chuckled. "And the problem is what?" she prompted.

"Val, the problem is, Keith Washington is…" She paused, looking for the right word. "…is Keith Washington."

"Gia, you're both single, consenting adults. You kissed a couple of times. The question is, where do you want this to go from here?"

"He makes me crazy and still I can't stop thinking about him. I know this can't go anywhere but—"

"Wait, why not?"

"You said it yourself, his father is running for mayor and I work as a community organizer. If the media found out this is going on, my credibility would be ruined. You obviously know him. Am I missing something?"

"Keith is exactly as he appears. He's a brilliant attorney who specializes in crisis management cases. He's charming, gorgeous and rich. On the flip side, he's a workaholic, extremely loyal to his family, single-focused and grumpy."

"Grumpy?" Gia queried.

"That's what his sister Prudence calls him. You know my friend Prudence. She married Michael Hunter from the Knights football team last year."

"That's right. I forgot she was also the mayor's daughter."

"Anyway, trust me, Keith is a good guy. He's honest and he's definitely not a player. So, are you gonna go for it?"

"He's drama."

"A lot of very successful relationships begin with a little drama."

"No," Gia said way too quickly to sound believable.

"He's also very determined."

"That part I believe. Okay, I guess I'd better get back to work now."

"Don't forget the Knights Ball tomorrow night."

Gia moaned. "I'm really not in the mood to hang out at a loud, crazy, headbanging party, Val."

"It's not going to be like that, trust me. This ball is to raise money for kids and it's gonna be totally wonderful. So you're going. I'll pick you up at seven."

"I gotta go. I'll call you tomorrow."

Gia drove on mental automatic back to the office. She parked her car in the usual spot beside the building then waited a few minutes. Her nerves were shattered. She still couldn't believe they'd kissed in public like that. What was she thinking? She'd kissed Keith Washington in broad daylight in the middle of Thirtieth Street Station. It was crazy. She opened the car door and hurried to the office.

Thankfully both Bonnie and Linda were too busy on the phone to actually see her so frazzled. They looked up quickly and waved as she passed by. She hurried to her office and pushed the door open. As soon as she sat down, her cell phone buzzed and vibrated. She pulled it out of her purse and looked at the caller ID. She knew the number instantly. It buzzed a second time. She waited for the voice mail to click on after the third ring. It didn't buzz again. The caller had hung up. She took a deep breath and exhaled slowly. There was a knock on the door. She looked up. "Yes, come on in."

Bonnie opened the door and peeked in. "Hi, you're back. Whoa, are you okay?"

"Yeah, fine," Gia said, playing off her distress. She shook her head. "It's just been a long, crazy day. So, is everything okay here?"

"Yeah, Danny's back. He's in Bill's office and we're just answering calls and stuffing information packets to get mailed out tomorrow. Anyway, I just came in to tell you that you had a strange phone call earlier. At first I just figured it was some nutcase because of what happened yesterday, but then," she said, handing Gia a piece of paper, "he said it was important that you call back."

Gia took the paper and read the number. "Thanks."

Bonnie nodded, then turned and walked out. Gia sat there shaking her head. Could this day get any crazier? She realized that she was losing control and she needed to get it back. She grabbed her cell and dialed Keith's phone number. She knew he was busy, but she also knew that if she called, he'd pick up. She wasn't ready to hear his voice. Texting would be better.

She sent him a simple message and as expected he texted her right back. She kept her request brief and to the point. She needed to meet him now. He agreed. There was no way she could bring him into this office again, so she suggested his office. He agreed. Good, she had a plan. Whatever this was going on between them it needed to stop before it got out of hand. She couldn't jeopardize the organization for him, no matter how tempting he was.

She stuffed the cell in her purse, getting ready to leave. Just as she stood, Bonnie came to the door again. "Hey, I need to run out for a few minutes. I shouldn't be long. If you need to reach me I'll be—"

"Um, wait. Before you go you have a visitor."

"A visitor?" she questioned, thinking it was Keith. "Who is it?"

"I've never seen him before. He said he was Sam Duncan."

Gia sat down slowly. Her heart thundered. *Sam Duncan*—the words bounced and rebounded in her head like a deranged pinball. It was impossible. It was a joke. The last time she saw her father was over six years ago when she turned her grandfather down. He and her grandfather had disowned her and neither had made any attempt to see or contact her since that day.

"Gia…" Bonnie said slowly.

"Um, yeah, umm, okay…" she muttered, then took a deep breath to try and calm her fraying nerves. She was coming apart standing right there. "Um, yeah, you can send him in. Thanks."

"Are you sure? I mean, you don't look, I don't know, convinced. I can send him away or have Bill come in, too."

"No, that's okay. I'm fine. Send him in."

"Yeah, you keep saying that, but seriously, girl, I don't think so. You look unnerved." Gia nodded. "Okay, I'll get him."

Gia looked at her desk and quickly around the office. It had been her grandmother's up until a few years ago, but now it was hers. Still, she hadn't changed much, if anything, at all. The books on the bookshelves were still her grandmother's, and the paintings and posters on the wall all belonged to her, too. Even the plant sitting in the corner was hers.

The only thing she added was the picture of her mother sitting on the desk in front of her. She was a child and they were on the beach building a sand castle. Her hair blew in the wind and she smiled, holding her mother tight around her neck, never wanting to let go again. It was a perfect moment frozen in time. A few years later her mother was dead and her world had fallen apart. Bonnie was right, hell yeah, she felt unnerved.

"Gianna."

Gia looked up to see her father standing in the open doorway. She exhaled slowly and half smiled. He hadn't changed a bit. He was tall, dark and handsome with just a hint of gray playing at his temples. He was still very fit and he still looked as fierce and unbending as he ever did. She swallowed hard. "Hello, Dad," she said softly.

"May I?" he asked before crossing the threshold and coming in.

She smiled. "I'm not so sure yet."

He walked in. "I see your sense of humor has improved."

"Actually, it hasn't," she said confidently.

He looked at her warmly and smiled that smile she loved seeing and seldom got to. "Gianna Duncan."

"Gia Duncan," she corrected quickly.

"Ah yes, it's Gia Duncan now," he confirmed. She nodded. He paused a long moment and looked her over, seeming to be memorizing her face; then he smiled pleasantly. "You are stunning, just as beautiful as your mother." He shook his head and walked farther into the office, looking around. "Julia's office," he said rather than asked. Gia nodded again. "Yes, I can tell. It looks just like her." He smiled, picking up the Chinese puzzle box on the bookcase and staring at it tenderly. He chuckled. "I could never figure out how to open this box even though your mother showed me a hundred times. I guess I never thought it was important enough to learn. I got this for her the day we met."

"I didn't know that."

"It's true. I'm glad you still have it." He looked at her and smiled, shaking his head. "You look just like your mother."

"Why are you here, Dad?" Gia asked, not sure she wanted to hear the answer.

He placed the small box back down on the shelf, then turned to look at her carefully. "How are you, Gianna?" he asked.

"I'm okay."

"Just okay?" he asked.

"I'm doing very well. I have my work. I have my friends and I have my—"

"Family," he said, interrupting.

"Yes, family, my grandmother," she said, knowing the painful subject was going to come up sooner or later.

"How is your grandmother?"

"Getting stronger every day, but I'm sure you already know that, don't you?"

He nodded so slightly that had she blinked she would have missed it. "I saw you today at the museum. No, I take that back. Your grandmother saw you, then pointed you out to me."

"I see."

"She misses you very much."

"I miss her, too. But nothing's changed."

"I guessed as much. I understand you're looking for additional funding for the organization. I'd be happy to give—"

"That's not necessary."

"You need the funding."

"I'll get the funding," she snapped back instantly.

He smiled and chuckled, shaking his head. "You are stubborn, and headstrong, just like your—"

"Father and grandfather, yes, I know."

Taken off guard, he laughed out loud. She smiled, too. "See, I was right, your sense of humor has definitely improved. So, tell me, you and Keith Washington."

She looked up quickly, then shook her head. "What about him."

"Is he the one?"

"I don't know what you're talking about," she said.

He nodded. "The day you were born I looked into your eyes and knew love for the first time in my life. You looked up at me and I knew I'd only have you for a short while and then one day a man would come into your life and take that place in your heart—my place. Is Keith Washington the one man who's gonna take my place in your heart?"

"It's business, just business. How did you know about Keith? Nobody knows."

"You're my daughter, Gianna. Trust me, I know."

She opened her mouth to speak but didn't know the words to say. "Dad, I—"

He held his hand up to stop her. "Change the office. Make it yours. She'd want you to." He nodded, turned and walked out.

Gia watched him go and the words still didn't come. What do you say to a man who gave you everything you ever wanted and then turned his back and disowned you? She walked to the door and out into the outer office. She watched him leave. Bonnie turned and looked at her questioningly. Okay, the day had officially gotten crazier. She turned and went back into her office.

She picked up the puzzle box, remembering how her mother had taught her to open it years ago. They had left messages to each other in the box. Pushing in, pulling out, turning and twisting, it unlatched and she opened it with ease. Inside was a folded piece of paper—the last note from her mother. She opened it and read the note, then quickly placed it back securely and returned the box to the shelf. She closed the door as the tears fell.

By six o'clock Bill and Danny had already left and Bonnie and Linda were headed out. Gia said her goodbyes, locked up, then went back into her office. She sat down and opened her laptop. She needed to get some work done and she needed not to think about her father right now. She opened one of the grant applications and read through what she had already written. It was good. It was adequate. But she knew she needed better. Her father was right about one thing—they needed the money. But pride wouldn't let her take his.

She went to work. An hour and a half into her writing, she was astonished at how exceptional the grant application was. It was flawless. All she needed now was to have the organization's attorney look it over and then… She stopped. Her heart jumped. "Keith," she whispered. She looked at her watch.

It had already been three and a half hours. She'd stood him up. She grabbed her cell phone and began texting.

Gia: I'm sorry, I was unavoidably delayed.

Keith: No problem. Anything I can do to help?

Gia: No. Can we meet later tonight?

Keith: Sure, my office still?

Gia: Yes, is 10:00 too late?

Keith: Not at all, I'll see you at 10.

Gia: Thanks.

Keith smiled for the first time that evening. He placed his cell phone back in his jacket pocket and looked at his watch. It was nine-fifteen. He had to make a move soon. He picked up his drink and took a sip. The hot strong espresso burned down his throat and felt good as he sat out in the cool evening air. He looked around his parents' deck, then out to the perfectly manicured backyard. Landscape and decorative tree lighting illuminated the area. It was the perfect relaxing setting, but he was still too tightly wound.

When it came to women he'd certainly had his share. Beautiful, stunning, elegant women surrounded him constantly. He liked them and they liked him. Life was very good. The initial feeling was always the same, but then they would inevitably want more than he was willing to give and he'd have to shut them down. So women came and then left. Life was still good.

But of all the others, none of them had given him the instant spark of connection that Gia had. The moment he saw her he felt it. And he knew for a fact that it was mutual. Now the idea of seeing her again excited him even more than he had expected. Kissing her had jump-started a hot burn of desire that he hadn't felt in a long time.

Her response to his kiss definitely attested to something happening between them. There was no hesitation, nor timidity. She gave just as ardently as he did. Passion met passion and had they been anywhere else there was no telling where that one kiss might have led them. He knew that she wanted him as much as he wanted her.

Keith looked up suddenly to see his brothers, Jeremy and Drew, standing in the kitchen doorway leading out to the back deck. "What?" he said, since they hadn't said a word, and even if they had, he hadn't been paying attention.

"I asked if the good news was work related or otherwise," Jeremy said, repeating what he'd said a few seconds earlier. He stepped all the way out onto the deck and took a seat next to Keith. Drew followed, taking a seat across from them. They each relaxed back into the heavily padded lounge chairs and looked at Keith.

"Actually I'm not quite sure yet," Keith said.

Drew glanced over at Jeremy. A second of knowing passed between them. "How'd it go picking up Mamma Lou?" Drew asked.

Keith looked at his brothers. "Why, what did you hear?"

Drew and Jeremy looked at each other. "Okay, what's going on with you?" Jeremy asked.

"Nothing," Keith quickly declared.

Drew chuckled. "Don't give us that. Pru gave you the name Grumpy, but tonight is was an understatement. You walk in here like it's the end of the world. Mom cooks one of your favorite meals and you pick at it like it's laced with poison. You barely speak and when Dad asked you a question earlier you had no idea what he was talking about. So the comment 'nothing' doesn't work. Answer the question. What's going on with you?"

"Is it Mamma Lou?" Jeremy asked quietly. "Is she after you?"

"No, she told me that she's here for someone else."

"Do you believe her?" Jeremy asked.

"I don't know. She may be trying to throw you off," Drew said.

"She's good," Jeremy declared while nodding.

"Mitigating factors would suggest differently," he said.

"What do you mean?"

"I believe her," Keith said.

"Who is her target?" Drew asked.

"It doesn't matter," Jeremy said, "as long as it's not one of us." He chuckled joyfully. "Well, my brothers, it looks like we are off the hook. We have successfully dodged the bullet this time. To the target, may we forever be missed." He held his espresso cup up to toast. Drew nodded and held his up, too.

They looked at Keith. He held his up, as well. They all took a sip.

"And what are we celebrating this evening, my dears?" Louise asked as she stepped out onto the deck, seeing the celebratory toast.

All three men began to choke.

Chapter 12

Gia hurried to the elevator and pressed the button. The doors opened instantly. She looked at the panel to see the top floor notated for Washington & Associates Law Firm. She pressed the button and silently the doors closed and the elevator began to ascend. She looked at her watch. It was two minutes before ten o'clock. A few seconds later the elevator doors opened. She stepped out and looked left, then right and straight ahead.

Half-frosted glass doors with logo and signage announced the law firm's executive suite. She stepped up to the doors and pushed through. One door gave with ease. A soft alarm began to sound and then shut off almost immediately. She turned and looked around. The lobby lights were slightly dimmed, but she could very easily see Keith walking toward her from down the corridor. "Good evening," he said, aiming the remote control in his hand at the alarm system again. It beeped a second time.

He continued to the glass door and flipped a lock in place, securing them inside. She was locked in. He turned and pressed a button on the remote control again. The lights in the immediate area brightened. He turned to her. His top button was undone and his tie was pulled loose just slightly, yet still keeping the perfect Windsor knot intact. She wondered what it would feel like to pull that tie free and open the rest of the shirt's buttons. She looked up into his eyes. It was as if he was reading her thoughts. "Hi, I'm glad you could come this time," he said, gazing at her.

Gia swallowed hard as she watched his lips move. The memory of his mouth on hers took her breath away. Her heart slammed hard and she began coughing.

"Are you okay?" he asked. She nodded. "Water?" he offered.

She shook her head. She barely recovered before realizing she hadn't spoken yet. "Hi, I'm fine. Good evening," she said. He smiled, showing bright white teeth and the sexiest smile she'd ever seen. She suddenly felt a shock of excited nerves tingle throughout her body. Locked in with Keith Washington—she wasn't sure if this was a good thing or a bad thing. She smiled weakly. "Thank you for seeing me so late."

"Are you sure you're okay?"

"Yes, I'm fine, just rushing to get here, never enough hours in a day." She looked around the lobby area, trying to compose herself. "Wow, these paintings are incredible."

Keith nodded proudly. "Thanks, I really treasure them. My grandmother painted them years ago."

"Emma Washington."

"Yes."

"She was very talented."

"Yes, I think so, too," he agreed.

There was a very pregnant pause as they looked at each other. "Um, listen, I'm really sorry about before. I hope I didn't keep you from anything too major."

"Just dinner with my parents," he said offhandedly.

"Oh, no, I'm so sorry," she said sincerely.

"It's okay, they were fine. We hang out together all the time. Being late for one dinner isn't gonna get me kicked out of the family will."

"You're lucky."

"What, having dinner with the family?" he asked. She nodded. He smiled. "You obviously don't know my family very well."

"No, I don't."

"Come, let's go to my office."

He led the way. She followed, watching every movement he made. Her gaze lingered on the smooth lay of his suit pants and his shirt still neatly tucked inside. *Stop it. Focus,* she mentally chided herself. He rounded the corner, walking with the sexy swagger of a man in control and who knew exactly what he wanted. She stared shamelessly at his rear as her mouth grew dryer and dryer and her heart began to pound some unrecognizable beat. *Good Lord, this man is too fine.*

"This is really nice," she said, distracting herself from watching him. "I really love the glass atrium in the lobby area. It seems very relaxing."

"Thanks, actually it's supposed to be. At least that's what the designer said. For some reason people don't always like coming to a lawyer's office."

"Imagine that," she joked as he walked into his office.

"Yeah, imagine that," he said.

It hit her in a rush of embarrassment. She'd just told him to imagine something just like at the station. Her train of thought, as well as his, quickly went to their kiss. He looked at her, smiling. She looked around his office. It was huge. "Wow, nice."

"Thanks. Please have a seat," he said, pointing to the sofa behind her. "Can I get you something to eat or drink?"

She walked over and sat down. "No, thank you, I'm fine. Well, actually, water would be great."

"Sure." He walked over to a panel behind his desk and pulled open what didn't even look like a door, let alone a refrigerator. He grabbed two bottles of water and brought them over. He handed one to her and kept the other as he sat on the chair angled beside the sofa.

"Thank you. I don't want to take up too much of your time. But I needed to say this in person—

a text, phone call or email wouldn't do. I think we need to get some things cleared up and boundaries set before we meet next week. This thing, the kiss in the station, the flirting, we need to put a stop to it. With the election right around the corner, neither one of us can afford a scandal. And we both know well enough there's no such thing as keeping secrets in this day and age."

"I see," he said as he opened his water and took a sip.

She watched his lips circle the rim and water flow down his throat. Her mouth suddenly felt like the Sahara Desert.

"What do you suggest we do exactly?" he asked. His deep, sexy voice seemed to tremble right through her.

Good Lord. The man oozed sex appeal and she was losing this battle with herself. All she could think about was sex, Keith and sex some more. "I suggest we keep our communication strictly professional," she answered, having no idea how she managed to get the words out.

"And you think we can do that."

"We're gonna have to," she said, trying to sound as decided as possible. He looked at her, and her stomach fluttered. The air in the room was immediately sucked out. "Keith, the looks, that's exactly what I'm talking about. The way you're looking at me right now. You have to stop."

He smiled. "I understand."

"Thank you." She stood abruptly. "I need to leave

now. Good night." She grabbed her things and hurried to the front lobby and stopped at the glass door. Keith was right behind her. "Open the door, Keith." She heard the beep of the alarm being shut off. She pulled the door handle, but the door didn't budge. "Keith."

He walked up behind her, reached around and unlocked the door. She grabbed the handle again. "Gia, what if, hypothetically, of course, I want more than a professional relationship with you?"

"Please don't," she warned, knowing this game. He wasn't the type of man whom woman said no to easily. He probably got whatever he wanted whenever he wanted it. She should have known he'd try to challenge her. But she was just as determined as he was. "This isn't going to happen."

"Why not?" he asked softly. "Why can't we—"

"You know why and I can be just as determined as you. So I'm not going to have a verbal sparring match with you." She whipped around. "We both know it builds to sexual tension and then…"

"Then?" he prompted with a seductive spark in his eyes. "Then what?" His suggestive smile made her stomach jump.

Damn him. Her body was already on fire. Now she could feel the moisture between her legs. She needed to get out of there now. She clamped her mouth closed, opened the water and took a sip, trying desperately not to chug the whole bottle. "Keith, what do you want from me?"

"I think you know the answer to that."

"Sex, is that all you want from me? Will that end this?"

"No."

She swallowed hard. There was something in his eyes that stilled her heartbeat. She'd known liars before, but this was no lie. He was telling her the truth. He reached his hand out to her. "Do you want me, Gia?"

The question was simple, but she still couldn't answer. Whatever she said or didn't say would surely have consequences. The question was, what was she willing to concede? She placed her hand on his, knowing this was the start of something she wasn't sure she could control. Standing, they stared into each other's eyes for what seemed like an eternity. There was just enough space between their bodies to add to the swell of temptation.

She turned and pulled the door open, then stopped. She looked at the dimmed lighting at the elevators, knowing exactly what was waiting for her—an empty, lonely life. She stepped back inside and latched the lock. She turned to see that he'd already turned to walked away. "Yes," she said, determined, "I do want you."

He turned around and walked back to her. He slowly leaned in. She met him halfway. Then, in an instant, a kiss exploded out of nowhere. She heard an impatient moan of abandoned passion and realized the sound was coming from her. The kiss was frantically out of control. Heads turned from side to side, mouths opened wider and wider, tongues darted in and out, caressing, protruding and demanding more. Deeper and deeper the ravenous kisses progressed until they were both gasping for air.

They panted breathlessly as a moment of clarity touched them. It wasn't too late to walk away. But the passion they felt was too strong. She shivered in need. He closed his eyes and dipped his head to her shoulder. "Gia, we can stop this now before…"

She nodded. "Yes, I know…" He stepped back, instantly opening the space between them. She reached out to touch his chest. The solid feel of his body excited her all over again. "…but I don't want to stop, do you?"

He smiled and shook his head. "No."

"Good," she said seductively, then began pulling the perfect Windsor knot apart. "Now, do you think we could get on to something more important?"

"Yeah, we can do that. Come on." He locked the doors again, took her hand and started walking backward to his office.

She then reached for his belt and slowly pulled it free. They went into his office and he kicked the door closed. He held tight to her waist as she began unbuttoning his shirt. When she finished she opened it wide and saw the luscious strength of his chest. She spread her fingers wide and touched him all over, then rolled his hardened nipple between her thumb and forefinger. A deep groan rumbled through his throat. She liked the sound. She reached up and pulled him close. She watched as he licked his lips. "Please tell me you have condoms here?"

He shook his head. "I don't, but my brother does in his office. I'll be right back."

She nodded as he slowly moved around her. Still holding on to the end of his tie, she pulled it free as he walked away. When he left she looked around. This office was truly amazing. It was part work area with a desk credenza, and part conference room with a table and chairs, and part living room with a comfortable sofa, chairs, a coffee table and full decorative accents. There were also two closed doors, which she assumed led to a bathroom and a vault of gold. She walked over to the desk and began to wonder.

"Second thoughts?" Keith said, walking back in.

Gia looked up but didn't turn around. "No, just thinking."

"About what?" he asked.

"How comfortable this all seems. I mean me being here with you. On paper it probably looks insane, but for some reason it feels so right." She turned around to see him. He stole her breath. "Who would have guessed you and me here now about to…"

"Make love." He finished her statement.

She nodded and leaned back on the edge of his desk. "Yeah, make love. I really don't know much about you, the real you."

He came over to lean back beside her. "My full name is Keith Emery Washington, my favorite color is purple, I listen to classical music in the car most times, but on really good days I listen to R & B and rap. I love to cook, but I seldom have the opportunity, I love jigsaw puzzles and I put clocks together as a hobby. I'm left-handed—the only one in the family, I drive an old beat-up truck on the weekend and I just bought an old farmhouse on three acres of land in Chestnut Hill. I've had a number of women in my life, but work is and will always be my main focus. And if this is as far as we go tonight, I'm okay with that." He stopped.

"I guess it's my turn now, huh?" she said, then stood up and stepped to stand in front of him, straddling his legs. She took the three condoms from his hand and tossed two on the desk. "I think maybe I'll tell you about me later. And for the record, this isn't as far as we go." She nibbled his earlobe and whispered, "Make love to me."

"I thought you'd never ask." He pulled her into his embrace and kissed her tenderly. His tongue slipped into her mouth and they savored the sweet essence of sensual pleasure. Moving his head from side to side, he deepened the kiss. The swelling sensation of arousal in the pit of her stomach dipped down between her legs, sending shock waves of heat through her body.

He held her waist, then pulled her even closer, gripped her rear to grind against his already hardened penis. Breathlessly she pulled back, breaking the kiss. She leaned her head back and he immediately began slowly ravishing her neck with tiny kisses, tender nips and long luscious licks.

Her body was well past the point of desire. She needed him now. It had been a long time since any man made her feel this wanted. She savored the feeling, knowing it would be a long time coming again. She felt the zipper pull down on her dress as Keith slowly pulled it from her shoulders. She stepped back. He eased it down her shoulders and waist, allowing her to step out.

She stood before him in stiletto heels, thigh-high stockings, panties and bra. He stared down the length of her body wordlessly. Suddenly she felt uneasy until he licked his lips and smiled lecherously. "I knew you were beautiful, but Gia, you are beyond stunning."

She smiled, slightly embarrassed. "Thank you."

"Turn around," he whispered.

She turned. He pulled her back between his legs as his hands came up to cup her beasts, circling her firm mounds with the palms of his hands paying special attention to her nipples. Already hardened, they ached to be released. As if reading her mind, he unsnapped the front clasp of her bra. He covered her breasts and began teasing her nipples. She rolled her head back, leaning on his shoulder and gasping in breathless pants.

"Does that feel good?" he whispered. She couldn't respond. Her mind was somewhere beyond cloud nine. "Do you want me to touch you?" She nodded. With one hand still caressing her breasts, the other dipped between her legs and circled the elastic lace of her waistband. Her legs trembled as she pushed back, grinding against the increasing hardness behind her.

He reached down, cupping her throbbing core.

She writhed as he played, tantalized and toyed with her swollen ache. She was wet and ready for him as his finger teasingly danced closer and closer. He slipped beneath the lace. Then one finger dipped and pushed inside, and she squealed. His second finger followed as his thumb stroked her nub over and over again. She squirmed and closed her eyes as the room began spinning dizzily. She moaned and groaned and whimpered and then finally she couldn't hold out any longer. She climaxed in a mind-blowing implosion. Her whole body shook and pulsated, convulsing between shock waves of orgasmic rapture.

Then in an instant she grabbed his hand and stepped away. She turned to him. Heaven help her, his hands were masterful, but she wanted the real thing. She pulled his shirt away and unzipped his pants, letting them drop to the floor.

His penis protruded through his boxer briefs. She touched him, grasping, then stroking his long, rock-hard shaft. She watched as he raked his lower lip with his white teeth. She had the power now. She leaned in and licked his hard nipple. His body shuddered and jerked. She did it again. This time he nearly convulsed. She liked this new power. She pulled his boxers down, freeing him completely. "Oh my," she whispered teasingly. "Now, what am I gonna do with you?"

"I have a suggestion," he rasped. His voice was thick and husky with desire. He pulled her close again. She grabbed a condom from the desk, opened it and placed it on his tip. Together they rolled and covered him. Now their bodies touched with her lace panties being the only barrier between them. His big strong hands grabbed the scant material and pulled them free. Then he cupped her rear and lifted her up onto his lap as he sat on his desk. She straddled him and then in one slow deliberate motion she eased down onto his hardness.

The tightness gave way to him within seconds. She burned, she tingled as she lowered herself even more, eventually taking all of him. Her body tightened to hold him in place. She arched her back, feeling completely filled. His mouth came to her breasts and his tongue licked and lavished her nipples as if they were dripping ice-cream cones. Her trembling hand held tight to his strong shoulders as she began gyrating her hips, moving up and down. He entered and exited in long sensual rhythmic strokes. She rode and he pumped until spasms of ecstasy took them over the top in a surge of passion. He poured into her and she held tight. But he was still hard. He picked her up. She wrapped her legs tightly with him still inside. He quickly moved back to the sofa and laid her down beneath him as he pressed deeper into her. Her nails bit into his shoulders. Her heart pounded as the surges came deeper, faster, harder and stronger until they both exploded again.

He rolled over, switching places with her. She now lay on top of him. Without protest she closed her eyes, waiting for the world to be reborn. There was no way it hadn't ended after that. She was completely drained. She had climaxed so many times she lost count. No man had ever done that to her. "That was…" she whispered eventually.

"Yes, I totally agree," he answered while stroking her back.

Both slipped into silence as their breathing synced as one and they fell asleep. She had no idea how long they slept. She awoke and reached for the bottled water. "I'll get that for you," Keith said.

"Thanks, did I wake you?"

"No, not really. Do you want another bottle of water?"

"No, this is fine." She got up and stepped away. Being naked didn't often bother her. But now wasn't one of those times.

He sat up. "Damn, woman, you take my breath away. Every inch of your body is mouthwatering. I swear I'm starving now."

She looked over her shoulder. "You think so, huh?"

"Oh, yeah, definitely."

"Do you have a private bathroom in here?"

"Yes." He pointed to one of the closed doors she'd noticed earlier.

She nodded. "I'll be right back." Moments later she returned. Keith was gone. She looked around and saw that his office door was now open. "Keith," she called out.

"Yeah," he said, coming back in and closing the door behind him. He had a bowl of fruit. "I thought you might be hungry."

"I am," she said with a glint in her eye. "Later."

He caught the look she gave him and instantly knew exactly what it meant. He placed the bowl of fruit on the disheveled desk and grabbed the second condom. She smiled teasingly. "Something different this time, I think."

He nodded slyly. "Oh, yeah, I got this." He grabbed a handful of cherries, marched over to her and picked her up. He placed her on the conference table, then sat down in a chair in front of her. She giggled, humored by his bold outrageous actions. He squeezed the cherries in his fist, and the sweet succulent juice ran down the front of her body. She squealed, seeing her body covered in red sweetness. He tossed the pits in the trash can, then moved his chair close. An instant later his mouth was all over her.

She lay back on top of the table and he fed like a condemned man. Her mouth, her neck, her shoulders, her beasts, her stomach and then he parted her legs. She gasped, arching up. He placed her legs on his shoulders and his hands on her breasts and ate until she was sated. Her body was weak and numb and her mind was beyond scattered.

Much later, dawn peeked in through the custom-fitted blinds. Gia took a deep breath, then released it as her body adjusted to the comfortable position. Then she realized she had fallen asleep and she was lying on top of a very naked man. And not just any naked man—Keith Washington. She opened her eyes and she felt his hand drift down to stroke her back and cup the sweet firmness of her rear. "Oh, no," she whispered.

Keith was obviously awake and had heard her. "Good morning," he said softly, barely above a whisper.

Gia closed her eyes tightly. "Please tell me this is just another dream."

"About me, how many have you had?"

"Never mind," she muttered.

"Okay, then it's a dream," he lied, "so lie back and relax."

She groaned. "How am I supposed to relax when I'm lying on top of the last man in the world I'm supposed to be with?"

"It could be worse," he said.

"How could this be any worse?" she asked, seeing the two condom wrappers on the pushed-aside coffee table and their clothes tossed on the chair.

"Well, you could be with the man Mamma Lou planned for you."

She sat up quickly and looked down at him. "What man?"

"My great-aunt likes to play matchmaker."

Gia closed her eyes and laid her bead back down on his chest. "I know about her infamous matchmaking skills. I hate to disappoint her, but I'm not interested in a long-term relationship of any kind."

"I agree, neither am I," Keith said.

"Good, then this was just a physical release."

"Exactly, a physical release," he repeated.

"You know no one can know about this, right?"

"Yes, of course. It would be very difficult to explain."

"Exactly, and since this only happened this one time…"

"Actually, it was a lot more than just one time."

"Well, technically yes, but we were together for just one night." He nodded. "I just don't think a lot of people will believe that we can still be professional, but we can."

"Yes, we can."

"So next week, with the meeting…"

"We will be completely professional. Our physical release will be set aside—business first."

She nodded. "It's almost daybreak. I'd better go."

"Unless of course you're up for another physical release."

"Yeah, that sounds good," she said, looking down at him.

"Yeah." Keith nodded. "I think so, too."

"But what if someone comes in here?" she said.

"They won't."

"You have a cleaning service. It's possible."

"Yes, but it's Saturday at six-thirty in the morning. No one's in my office at that time except me."

"And me," she said, smiling.

"Oh, yeah, definitely you," he agreed, pulling her closer.

Gia delved into Keith's kiss with all the fervent passion inside her. Her body was ready because she knew this was definitely going to be the last time this happened. After this physical release, there was only one thing to do. Stay as far away from Keith Washington as possible, but for right now she'd enjoy him.

Chapter 13

Keith: Miss me already, don't you?

   Keith: Silence?

   Keith: It's like that, huh?

   Keith: Not tempted? Not even a little?

"No," Gia said adamantly to herself as soon as she looked at the caller ID number. It was Keith texting her again. She was tempted and he knew it. He also knew what she was doing. This was his fourth text message and she still refused to respond. She needed to end what she had started. One night, that's all, she promised herself. She had had her physical release and now it was time to move on. She couldn't chance being with him again no matter how much she wanted to. That's what they had promised. She had to be professional.

Saturday morning and afternoon Gia did everything she could think of to keep busy all day long. She visited her grandmother for breakfast, she did laundry, ran errands, went grocery shopping, cleaned her house and then hand-washed her car. The more mundane the chore, the better. She knew as soon as she stopped motion, she would think about Keith. But not only did she have memories of him to contend with, she also had Mamma Lou to deal with. She did not have time for her matchmaking drama. And whoever she had in mind for her would be most sadly disappointed.

So when her cell phone rang at three o'clock and she saw it was her friend Val she was overjoyed. "Hey, Val, what's up?"

"Hey, girl, I just called to check on you," Val said. "The last time we talked, life was getting complicated. How's that going?"

Gia half chuckled. "Girl, you don't even want to know."

"Oh, Lord, sounds like complicated got crazy complicated," Val said with a laugh. "What happened?"

"You're right. It got crazy complicated and then some. After I spoke to you I went back to the office. Everything was cool and then my dad showed up out of the blue. He just stopped by like it was no big deal."

"You've got to be kidding me. For real, how long has it been since you've spoken?" Val asked.

"It's been almost six years. But wait, there's more.

I ran into my grandfather at the mayor's Initiative Conference."

"Okay, that's just crazy," Val said.

"Yeah, but that's not the craziest, complicated part. I decided to call Keith and tell him that whatever was going on between us had to stop. I went over to his office late last night and I wound up spending the night with him and then…"

"Whoa. Whoa. Whoa. Wait a minute, back up. You just can't breeze through something like that and not give me details. You and Keith Washington spent the night together in his office?"

"Yes," Gia said softly.

Val laughed happily. "Good for you, it's about time."

"Girl, the man was amazing, but now it just seems so impulsive. I'm sure he does that all the time, but I—"

"Actually, I'd bet my entire 401K you're wrong. I told you, Keith is a good guy. He's not about all that player stuff. Yeah, he's had his share of women, but it's not like that with him. He doesn't play games and I've known him a long time."

Gia thought about what Val said for a brief moment. Everything about Keith seemed to prove true. He had never lied to her and he wasn't trying to take advantage of her.

"Listen, right now I need to get out of here and do something to keep my mind off this. So I have a great idea. Let's go out tonight and do an early dinner and catch a movie."

"Yeah, we're definitely going out tonight, but we're not doing dinner and a movie. We have tickets for the ball."

"Tickets for what ball?" Gia asked.

"I reminded you last week and then again on Thursday, so please don't tell me you forgot about the Knights Children's Benefit Ball at the Grand Hotel tonight."

"Oh crap, I forgot," Gia groaned.

"No excuses, you're coming with me," Val said firmly. "It's the team's bye week, so they're not playing on Sunday. That means we'll be partying all night with every football player on the team. And here's the best part. We have the inside track because of Prudence. And you know you need this. We both do."

Gia rolled her eyes. The last thing she felt like doing was going to a big crowded party with a bunch of football players. "Val…"

"Don't even say it. As many political events as I've attended with you, you, missy, are going to this with me. It's black-tie."

"I don't have anything to wear."

"Now I know you're lying. You have more clothes than Prudence, and she's a department store fashion buyer."

"Okay, okay, I give up."

"Gia, it's not a firing squad. It'll be fun. You said you wanted to get your mind off of your crazy drama. This is the perfect distraction—big, strong, gorgeous men. Believe me, this is gonna be the party of the decade. I'll see you at seven."

"Okay, seven o'clock. See you then."

Gia closed her cell phone and went into her bedroom. Hanging out late tonight wasn't exactly what she had planned, but she did promise Val weeks ago that she'd go with her. She sat down on her bed and turned her television on to the weather channel. Midway through the evening's forecast her cell phone beeped again. She picked it up and saw that it was another text message.

Keith: Tonight?

Gia smiled slyly, enjoying the private one-sided conversation. She bit at her lower lip, tempted by his single word. She exhaled the breath she'd been holding and shook her head. One typed word. Apparently that was all it took for her to abandon a promise to her friend and consider spending another night in his arms. Granted, if tonight was anything like the night before, she'd be dancing on cloud nine five minutes after seeing him.

Tempted or not, of course she wouldn't do it. Still, everything about him was so right it scared her. He was amazing. She lay back on her bed, staring at the ceiling. She instantly began thinking about his touch and how he'd made her body feel. But that was the past. It wouldn't happen again no matter how much she wanted it to.

Keith glanced up in the rearview mirror as he drove up to valet parking. This wasn't what he had expected to do tonight, but he didn't have much of a choice. He had given his word to his sister and brother-in-law and he wasn't about to break it. He turned his music off and got out just as the valet parking attendant approached, handing him a ticket stub. He placed it in his jacket pocket and proceeded inside as cell phones and professional cameras flashed in his face.

Keith followed the hotel's signage pointing the way to the Philadelphia Knights Children's Benefit Ball. The event started at eight-thirty and it was already getting crowded. He spoke to a few people and then continued to the ballroom's entrance. An explosion of black and silver balloons arched across the double doors. He handed over his invitation and received a silver band around his wrist.

"Hey, Grumpy, thank you for coming to support the kids."

Keith turned to see his sister, Prudence, walking up to greet him. He was still having a hard time getting used to seeing her rounded belly protruding out so far. But at six months pregnant, she still looked great. "Hey, Pru, everything looks amazing."

"Oh, stop lying. I know this place looks like a million other events at a million other hotels, but trust me, tonight is going to be very special. Are Drew and Jeremy here yet?"

Keith looked around. "I haven't seen them yet. But with all the women out front and in here, I'm sure they're on their way."

Prudence hooked her arm in his and walked back

toward the ballroom's entrance. "I'm glad you came a little early. I wanted to talk to you about Dad. The news is getting a little rough. He's getting attacked all the time. He says he's fine, but I don't know. Maybe it's my hormones and I'm losing it, but I'm worried. Is he okay, I mean with the reelection? Is he gonna win again?"

"He's fine, Pru, and he will be reelected. Trust me. I'm doing everything I can to make that happen, but honestly the bottom line is he's the best man for the job."

Prudence smiled with relief. "You don't have to sell me. He's got my vote and quite a few others," she promised.

"Good. Now how are you feeling?"

Prudence rubbed her belly and smiled. "I feel fantastic. I've never been happier in my life, except Mother is driving me crazy."

"First grandchild," Keith said.

"I get the whole first grandchild thing, but she's driving me nuts. Why don't you get engaged and married? That'll distract her for my last few months and I can get a little peace."

"Yeah, okay. I'll make sure to do that," Keith said, looking around as people began entering the ballroom. The event had officially begun. "Looks like it's started. Shouldn't you be playing hostess or something?"

"Yeah, but right now I want to hear more."

"More about what?" he asked.

"Does that comment mean you're seeing anyone special and the possibility of marriage is on the table?" she asked. Keith just smiled. He seldom talked about his personal life, and that always drove Prudence crazy. She already knew he wasn't going to answer her. "That's okay. You don't have to answer. I already heard about your drive to Thirtieth Street Station."

Keith looked at her quickly. "What did you hear?"

Prudence chuckled, always enjoying teasing her older brother. "By the way, Mamma Lou's here and you know what that means. As a matter of fact, I believe she's got a nice surprise for you."

"What surprise?" Keith asked with concern. Prudence smiled and walked away. "Pru. Pru. Prudence, what surprise?" he repeated.

Prudence chuckled while waving and heading to the front table. "You'll see. Have a good time. See you later, big brother."

Keith stood a moment and just shook his head. Mamma Lou—that's all he needed right now. An instant later he looked around as if he'd just been targeted. He knew she was coming tonight, but she'd said that she was focused on someone else, on Gia. His body suddenly tensed. The thought of Mamma Lou matching Gia with another man made the muscles in his neck tighten.

He walked over to one of the bars and ordered a drink. He stuffed a generous tip in the glass jar, then leaned back and looked around aimlessly. He was losing his focus. It bothered him that Mamma Lou was playing matchmaker with Gia, he could admit that, but why it bothered him, was another thing altogether.

Gia. The effect she was having on him was starting to concern him. He thought about her way too much. And every time he saw her, the feelings he had got stronger and stronger. For the last few days she was all he thought about. She was always there in the back of his mind and he knew exactly what that meant. No, he quickly denied it. This wasn't happening to him. With his father's campaign and his busy law practice, he didn't have time for love. It was just a sex thing. But the truth was, he'd been thinking about her way before their night together.

He saw his mother and father walk in and instantly thought about their love story. His father always said that he fell in love in an instant. One glance across a crowded courtroom was all it took. Keith smiled, remembering the first time he saw Gia. She took his breath away. And now his great-aunt was going to match her with someone else. It was just a physical release, he told himself again. But it didn't matter, in his heart he knew better. He pulled out his cell phone and texted one word.

He watched as his parents walked over to a table. He saw Mamma Lou talking with Prudence, Val and… He shook his head, only half-believing his eyes. Gia was here. His eyes locked on her instantly. The sight of her dressed in royal blue scorched a heated path straight down his body. Her hair was swept up, held by a studded clip. She smiled graciously and laughed with ease. She was mesmerizing and his fingers itched to touch her again.

Just then, Rick Renault walked up to the small gathering. He shook hands with his father, then hugged his great-aunt, his mother, his sister, Val and with Gia he lingered too long.

Rick had a serious reputation for breaking hearts. His romantic prowess with women was legendary. Like his brother-in-law, he was a quarterback with the Knights football team, and women of all races, ages and economical backgrounds usually fell head over heels in love with him instantly. The problem was, Rick was a serious player.

Keith watched their interaction closely. Rick said something. Everyone laughed, Gia smiled and Rick looked right at her. Keith knew exactly what he was thinking. That was enough. He slammed his drink down on the bar, nearly tipping it over, and then he headed right to them. The arrowlike determination on his face was unwavering. He pulled out his cell phone and sent one last text message.

"Whoa, look at this crowd. Are we late?" Gia asked.

"No, we're right on time. I guess all these people came early. O-M-G, look at this place," Val said excitedly. She excused herself repeatedly as they moved around the massive crowd of guests looking for Prudence.

"I know. It's like the crowd is growing every minute. This is insane, all this just to see football players. It's crazy."

"Not just football players, the Philadelphia Knights. They're the champions. Okay, there she is by the entrance to the ballroom," Val said. "Come on, let's go, this way."

Gia followed as Val eased around the side and came to the table in front of the main ballroom. She called out and waved. A very pregnant woman turned, smiled and motioned her over. They hugged. "Hey, you're here. Thank you so much for coming."

"Are you kidding? I wouldn't have missed this craziness for the world. Look at all these people. I had no idea it was going to be this crowded. Here are our invitations. You remember my friend Gia Duncan."

Prudence nodded and smiled. "Sure, yes, of course. Hi, Gia. Val told me you were coming with her tonight. Thank you so much." They hugged also. "You are gonna have a great time tonight. There are so many great guys here."

"Thank you for inviting me," Gia said louder because of the noise around them. "It looks like it's gonna be an awesome event."

"I hope so. It's to raise money for the Knights Children's summer camps. Come on, let's go inside. Believe it or not, since the band started playing it's a lot quieter in there." Prudence walked over and handed the two invitations to the woman standing at the door and received two silver wristbands. Val and Gia put them on, and then followed Prudence into the ballroom. Inside wasn't nearly as packed.

Prudence led, Val and Gia followed. She introduced them to several football players and members of the stadium front-office staff. They laughed and talked and then after a while a man came up behind Prudence and wrapped his arms around her waist. "Hey, babe, are you doing okay?"

"Yeah, fine," Prudence said. "You remember Val. And this is another friend, Gia Duncan."

Michael smiled the winning smile he was famously known for. "Ladies, welcome. You both look amazing."

"Hey, Michael," Val said, hugging him warmly.

"Val, what's up? Thanks for coming. Gia, it's good meeting you. Thanks for coming and supporting the kids. Now, I've already told the guys to be on their best behavior. I also told them that my wife had invited a couple of her friends, so there are a couple of guys dying to meet you ladies."

"Cool," Val said happily. Gia just shook her head.

"Come on, I want you to meet my great-aunt," Prudence said. Val followed. Gia hesitated a split second. "Hey, Mamma Lou, are you having a good time?"

"Yes, these football players are just as sweet as they can be. I can barely sit down when one of them isn't grabbing me up to dance again. I'm having the time of my life."

Prudence laughed. "Great. Mamma Lou, you remember my friend Val from the wedding, and this is another friend—"

"Gia, I didn't know you were coming tonight," Louise said.

"You know each other?" Prudence said.

"Of course, I've known Gia since she was a babe in my arms. She came to pick me up at the train station yesterday, but Keith was already there. And the funniest thing—"

"Hi, Mamma Lou," Gia said quickly while kissing her cheek. She needed to put a swift end to her train station comment. Of course she had seen Louise Gates as soon as she walked into the huge ballroom. An eighty-year-old woman on the dance floor with two football players was hard to miss. She thought about Keith's matchmaking warning and immediately figured that the mystery man might be here, as well. The last thing she wanted was to be matched up. But right now she didn't have much of a choice.

Her cell phone beeped. She opened her purse and checked the text message, knowing exactly who the message was from. When she saw the one word her stomach twitched.

Now!

Chapter 14

"Good evening."

The deep, sexy voice resounded right beside her. Everyone smiled happily. Gia looked up, stunned. She turned slowly. Keith was staring straight at her and he didn't look happy. He looked menacing, but sexy as hell. Then, instantly, his expression changed as if it were never there. His family greeted him warmly with joyful hugs, loving kisses and unending smiles. He reciprocated generously. Gia watched as he took just a few seconds with each family member, but she could see they all felt special. Then he hugged and kissed Val like another sister.

When he addressed her, she smiled, giving nothing away. "Hi, Keith, it's good to see you again."

"Gia, how are you?"

As soon as he spoke, her heart thundered and her knees went weak. Everyone watched attentively. She did her best to appear unfazed, but inside she was a category-five hurricane. "I'm well, thank you. And you?" she said as pleasantly as she could.

He smiled and nodded. "I'm good. I'm surprised. I didn't expect to see you this evening. I'm glad you came. We have a meeting next week in my office," he said to the others.

The words *in my office* nearly knocked her off her feet. She nodded repeatedly. "Yes, we do. We're looking forward to it."

An instant sensual heat swept through her body when he leveled the last look at her. Then he casually turned to Rick Renault standing beside her. They shook hands and did the brother hug, joking briefly about the stunning women standing with them. Everyone laughed. She observed Keith and Rick. They didn't seem like the best of friends, but it was obvious that they knew each other well.

Keith had done exactly as she asked—he was professional. The man who had curled her toes the night before and licked her like a lollipop barely acknowledged her existence. Yeah, sure, it was what she had wanted. They were going to be professional in public, but now she wasn't so sure she liked it.

After a while the conversation changed to the weather, travel, family, sports and finally back to the benefit. Prudence excused herself to introduce Val to someone, and Marian and Blake moved on to mingle and speak with another couple. Mamma

Lou, Rick, Keith and Gia were left talking about the amazing turnout and the beautiful decorations and dreamlike atmosphere.

While they talked, Gia took the opportunity to look at Keith more closely. There was no other way to put it, the man was gorgeous. Wearing the perfect tuxedo, he oozed sex appeal and it fit the body she knew all too well with style, class and exceptional taste. No lie, he could have stepped right off the cover of any fashion magazine.

Keith's looking as good as he did, a parade of women passed by constantly. They openly stared at both Rick and Keith with one thing on their minds. Gia tried not to be affronted, but it was impossible not to take offense. They sashayed by wearing navel-dipped cleavage and dresses barely covering their butts. The statement was being made and it was impossible to miss. Keith and Rick were targeted. The women made their intentions known and it was obvious they didn't care who either man was with.

The tempo of the music changed to something much slower. A female singer took the microphone and began singing an old-school favorite. Her voice was smooth and promising. The lights dimmed and the dance floor filled with couples moving in to dance more intimately.

"Gia," Rick began, "would you like to dance?"

Gia opened her mouth to respond, but before she could say anything Keith answered for her. "Actually, Rick, the lady is with me this evening. I believe this is my dance." He held his hand out. Gia took it, smiled at Mamma Lou, nodded to Rick and then followed Keith out onto the dance floor. He maneuvered them to the very center so that they were completely surrounded.

Keith raised her hand, his thumb pressed gently into her palm. Then he wrapped his arm possessively around her waist and drew her into his embrace. He caressed her bare back tenderly, making every nerve ending in her body quiver. She knew she needed to break this spell, but for right now this was all she wanted—to be in his arms just one more time.

Several women turned in their direction. Some smiled with warm acceptance, others with envious green. But she didn't care. How can you focus on anything else when your body is on fire? "Thank you for that," she said, barely recognizing her own voice.

"For what?" he asked.

"Rescuing me. I have a feeling that Rick Renault is the man Mamma Lou wanted to match me up with tonight. She's your aunt and I know she means well, but there's no way he and I are compatible. We wouldn't last a week in the same room."

Keith smiled inwardly. This was exactly what he needed to hear. And he knew she was right. Mamma Lou had completely missed the mark matching Rick and Gia together. They were complete opposites with absolutely nothing in common. Rick was also the least likely man to be matched with anyone. He was, by his own admission, professed to be a bachelor for life. But instead of saying anything, Keith allowed Gia to think otherwise. "You're welcome."

"I love this song and she sings it really well. It always reminds me of what love is supposed to feel like."

"Have you ever been in love?" Keith asked.

"No, not really. At least I don't think so."

"If you don't think so, then how would you know?"

"When I think of love I think of being in perfect peace. Not that he will be perfect or anything like that, but he'll be perfect for me. We'd be completely comfortable together. There'd be no need for secrets because everything would be open."

"What does that look like, the perfect man for you?"

"I'd think of him all the time and I wouldn't be able to stop smiling. Seeing him would make my heart skip a beat and my knees weak. His touch would both comfort and thrill me. And his voice would send shivers through my body. And..." she added, then stopped. She realized that everything she'd just said was exactly what she felt with Keith.

"And what?" he questioned.

"And did I tell you that you look very handsome tonight?"

"Thank you. And you look ravishing," he whispered.

"Thank you," she said quietly.

"Although," he began, dipping closer for her ears only, "I think I prefer you as you were last night."

"Naked?" she asked.

He leaned back, looked into her eyes, then gripped

her closer, spreading his fingers wide against her lower back and pressing her closer. "Yeah, that'll work."

She blushed shamelessly. "Right back at you."

"Are you tempting me, Ms. Duncan?"

"Of course not," she said innocently, licking her lips and feeling the burn of her body suddenly overwhelm her. "That would be wrong, particularly given our agreement."

"Yeah, very wrong," he whispered, moving his hips to grind against her. She felt the stiffness of his penis press close. She gasped, instinctively holding him tighter. He was masterful, knowing exactly what it took to excite her.

He leaned back slowly. Their eyes connected. They said everything there was to say without speaking a single word. He licked his lips and she shivered. He smiled, knowing the effect he had on her. He dipped her hips, pressing his thigh between her legs. It was mind-blowing and arousingly sensual. He stroked the full length of her back, and every thought she tried to hold instantly shattered. It was as if they were making love all over again. This time they were in the center of a crowded room surrounded by hundreds of people. This was getting to be too much. She had no idea how she was going to walk off this floor when the song ended.

"Keith."

"Yes," he whispered.

She couldn't respond. Her mind was a tattered mass of scrambled images from the night before. All she could focus on was their bodies entwined in the intimate dance of lovemaking and looking into his eyes as he sent her body skyrocketing to unimaginable climaxes.

"Um, I think we're getting in trouble again."

"Is that a bad thing?" he asked.

She wanted to say yes immediately, but she knew she couldn't. But then again… Her heart pounded like a snare drum. He was holding her just right and moving his body against her, and between the two she was losing the battle. "Keith," she moaned again. He dipped his mouth to her ear and tenderly kissed her lobe. "I think maybe…" His hot moist breath nearly vaporized her skin. Breathing was almost impossible. "Maybe…"

"Yes."

"Um, I was thinking, maybe we can…"

"Make love right here, right now," he suggested.

"Probably not the best idea," she said, knowing he was joking.

"Are you sure?" he asked humorously.

She smiled and leaned back. They laughed quietly as he held her slightly away. The song was coming to an end and they both knew that they needed to calm their emotions down. Gia sighed heavily. "What in the world am I going to do with you?"

"Keep me," he said offhandedly.

She smiled. "Oh, definitely that." They smiled.

"So, when, where?" he asked her.

She shrugged. "I don't know how we can do this."

"Maybe we should start by just getting out of here."

"Yeah, that sounds good, but I came with Val. She drove."

"No problem. I'm sure Val will understand."

"Yeah, I know she will." Gia glanced around the dance floor, seeing the many couples around them. Most were football players with young "barely dressed in anything" women dancing impossibly close. Then she spotted Rick dancing with Mamma Lou. "Uh-oh, that's not good. Looks like Mamma Lou gave up on me and now he's next. Do you think he knows he's in trouble?"

Keith glanced over to see the odd pair enjoying their dance as women of all ages stared enviously at them. He chuckled. "If he doesn't, he will soon enough."

"You realize, Mrs. Gates, they'll be taking my player card for this," Rick said, releasing her to slowly turn around, then back to him again.

Louise smiled brightly. "Call me Mamma Lou, dear. Everyone does. And you're not a player. You're just a wonderful man who hasn't found the right woman yet. But no worries, that will change soon enough."

Several women stood along the side of the dance floor watching them enviously. Rick knew they stared and he knew exactly what they wanted—him. "And don't you even look in their direction. We both know they don't mean you any good. They'll just take half your money and make a mess of your life."

Rick smiled and chuckled as he held Louise gently and carefully glided her around the floor. "Yeah, but you have to admit, they do look good in those dresses."

Louise glanced over to see the women openly staring and nearly drooling at her dance partner. She chuckled. "What dresses? I see two stickers and a rubber band."

Rick laughed out loud while shaking his head. There was no way in his wildest dreams that he would think he'd be on the dance floor with an eighty-year-old woman while in a room filled with very willing good times waiting to happen. But here he was. And even more amazing, he had no idea how he had let this wonderful old lady talk him into putting the moves on Gia just to get Keith to step up, but she did that, too. But to her credit, as soon as Keith took Gia's hand he knew Louise Gates was right. They had love in their eyes.

"I have to admit, you were right, they do look good together."

Louise nodded. "Yes, they do. Now, Rick, tell me about you. I want to know everything. "

"Okay, let's see, I'm a football player for the Philadelphia Knights. I'll be a free agent when my contract expires at the end of this season. I'd like to head back to my hometown."

"Where's home?" she asked.

"I was born and raised in New Orleans, Louisiana."

"Oh, I have quite a few very good friends down in Louisiana," Louise said, smiling and nodding as Rick continued. She listened closely, knowing of course that he'd be absolutely perfect for her next little project.

Chapter 15

They left the ball at separate times, him in his car and her in a cab. They met up at the diner. He was there when she walked in. The diner's lights were bright and, dressed in a stylish evening halter dress and five-inch stiletto heels, she might have seemed completely out of place, but for some reason she felt right at home sliding into his usual booth. "This is so not the way I thought this evening was going to end," Gia said.

"It's not over yet," Keith promised.

"I meant being here with you," she said softly. Keith smiled. Gia's stomach tumbled. The man could rock her world without even saying a word. She picked up the menu and flipped through without paying much attention. He picked up his menu, too. She smiled to herself.

It had taken her twenty-eight years to feel this alive, and for the first time in a long while she was deliriously happy. After all the flirting and foreplay on the dance floor, they hadn't done anything when they were finally alone together. Of course they weren't really alone.

"What can I get you?" Gladys asked.

"Are you hungry?" Keith asked.

"No, not really."

"Dessert," he said.

She smiled and nodded. "Perfect."

"Cake or pie?" Gladys asked.

"Pie," Keith and Gia said together, then laughed.

Gladys shook her head. "Ya'll been having a little too much fun tonight?"

"Not nearly enough," Keith said.

"I agree," Gia added.

"I guess those notes ya'll passed the other night really did the trick. A'ight, what kind of pie ya'll want, darlings? We have apple, cherry, blueberry, lemon meringue and Boston cream."

"Cherry," Keith said.

Gia nodded, smiling knowingly. "Definitely cherry."

Gladys nodded and walked away. She returned a few minutes later with two huge slices of cherry pie and two cups of tea.

Keith and Gia ate pie and drank tea while Keith talked about his father's economic plan for the city.

He explained in detail their ideas. Gia listened, both impressed and delighted.

"Wow, it sounds wonderful. But will it happen?"

"It already is. The mayor has everything already in place. He's going to meet with the council to finalize the details in the next few weeks."

"They don't know about the plan?"

"They know the general basics, but unfortunately they aren't the easiest seated council to work with. In most cases the mayor has to circumvent certain obstructions to get anything done."

"That's not exactly ethical, is it?"

"It's legal."

"What if someone finds out?"

He smiled at her. "Yes, what if?"

"Chairman Jameson," she said, knowing that's who he meant.

He nodded. "Yeah, your boy. He'd be very interested in this."

"No, not my boy," she defended quickly. "I know it seems to you that OCC and Jameson are tight, but it's not true. Bill and Lester are friends. Lester and Bill's dad grew up in the same neighborhood. When Bill and his dad lost their money in that Ponzi scheme, Lester helped his father out."

"So you owe him?"

"No, I don't own him and OCC doesn't owe him."

"You might want to check with Bill about that."

"Bill's all right. He just has family issues. He lost almost everything and being penniless isn't his style. His half sister, Bonnie, still has her trust fund and inheritance from their grandparents, so every day it's a reminder that he's broke."

"Money has a way of making smart people do desperate things."

Her eyes narrowed. "Are you trying to warn me about something, Keith?"

"Would you listen to me if I did?" he asked.

"Probably," she said, wondering just how serious he was.

Keith nodded. "Consider yourself warned."

She thought about what he said and the whole conversation. But she quickly dismissed his implication. Keith was still a wild card in all this. "Is that all?"

"That's all I have for you right now."

"Keith, if you know something…"

"I do. I know you are stunning this evening. I know I'd love nothing more than to release that bow and have your dress drop to my feet. I know that sitting here talking to you about politics is the last thing I want to be doing with you. And I know that you make my body burn and I can't stop thinking about you, every day, every hour and every minute."

"What, not every second?" she asked playfully.

He nodded. "I have a feeling that's coming very soon."

"I know that feeling."

"Good. I'd hate to be alone in this."

"You're not."

"Ya'll want something else from the kitchen?" Gladys asked.

"No, I'm good, thanks. It was the best pie I've ever eaten."

"I'll pass that on to Twister," Gladys said, then sashayed away.

"So, tell me about the rest of your family," Gia began. "I know a lot about your father. What about your mother? We've met, but what's she really like?"

Keith smiled. "Marian Washington is a no-nonsense family court judge who loves children and the law. She protects them both equally and tries her best to keep families together. She's soft-spoken and even-tempered. It takes a lot to push her buttons, but when she's upset you'll know it."

Gia's eyes widened. "She sounds fierce."

"No, no, not at all. She's the sweetest woman ever."

"Spoken like a dutiful son."

"All right, tell me about your mother and growing up," Keith said. "You lived in Boston for a while, right?"

Gia stopped smiling and nodded. Keith reached over and placed his hand on hers. "Along with my grandmother, my mother is my hero. We didn't have a long time together, but the time we had was magical. I remember being very happy and then she died and I wasn't anymore. Afterward, I lived with my father and grandparents. When my father remarried I went to a boarding school in Boston. I ended up staying there."

"What about your grandmother?" he asked.

"I was told my grandmother didn't want anything

to do with me. I believed it. I could never understand why or what I had done to make her not want to see me. So, growing up, I always felt disconnected. Funny, saying it now sounds so strange.

"When I graduated from college I contacted my grandmother. I guess I just wanted to meet her as an adult. She was nothing like I expected or was told. She told me she loves me and she knew everything about me. She even sneaked in and went to my high school and college graduations. I asked her why she never wanted to see me after Mom died. She told me that she'd been told that I never wanted to see her again.

"Money has a way of making people different. I confronted my father and grandfather about the lies they told me. Long story short, they didn't want her to influence me. I told them it was too late and I had no intention of working with them. They cut me off monetarily. You know, it's funny, when you're used to having money, life is a lot easier. Then when you don't have it anymore you learn that money isn't everything."

Keith nodded slowly. "Money sometimes has a way of magnifying the worst in people."

"True. Anyway, my grandmother and I got closer and when she had the heart attack I moved back here to Philly to take care of her. Then she got sick again and I took over her position at OCC."

"You have a law degree, so why community service?" he asked.

"Why not?" she answered quickly. "The best answer I can give you is that I like helping people, but more as a whole, not necessarily one person at a time like in law or social work."

"The greater good," he suggested.

She smiled and nodded. "Yeah, that's exactly it, the greater good." She looked into his eyes, and the feeling was back instantly. But what she saw warmed her heart just as much. The same feeling was reflected in his eyes. "Keith, what do you think this is, us here, now and before?"

Keith knew exactly what she meant. "Right now this is us getting to know each other without all the goggling and newspaper articles. And before, well, before was…" He smiled seductively. "This is nice, though, very nice."

She nodded. He was right. "Yes. This is nice, talking with you like this. I like it, not that before wasn't great, it's just…"

"What?" he asked.

She leaned in closer and lowered her voice. "Having crazy, all-night-long, multiple orgasmic and nonstop sex with you the first time we were alone together was not good," she said, then paused. "Wait, don't get me wrong, you were amazing, you know you were amazing. The sex was phenomenal and being with you makes me crazy happy, but…" she said, then looked away. He stroked the palm of her hand gently just as he'd done on the dance floor. Her stomach instantly jumped. "But that wasn't me. I still can't believe we did that, that I did that. It was too fast, too soon."

He nodded. "Yes, it was fast. And I have a feeling that no matter how much we might want to slow this down, it's out of our hands. But I promise we'll go at your pace."

"I guess we could just be friends, professionals," she said. Although his expression never wavered, she knew her words had affected him. Truth be told, they affected her, too. He was right. This was more than either of them had expected. "I don't know if I'm ready for more than that."

He didn't speak for a few moments. Then he nodded. "Whenever you're ready, come find me. I'll be waiting."

Chapter 16

It was her suggestion and it was without a doubt the dumbest thing she'd ever come up with. Seven days, one week since they had talked all night in the diner and the only thing she got were brief phone messages asking how she was doing. She saved them all, of course. Playing them over and over again was childish but she needed to hear him, even if it was just a recording. Just hearing his voice sent shivers down her body. She grabbed her phone in a desperate attempt to clear her head. "Hey, Val, it's Gia, are you busy?"

"No, not at all, just catching up on some work."

"On a Sunday morning?" Gia said.

"You know me, forever saving humanity by righting the wrongs of the world and putting away one nutcase at a time. You know the drill," she said, "superhero stuff."

"Woman, you are so dramatic," she laughed.

"Yeah, yeah," Val chuckled.

Gia laughed. "Okay, superhero, question. What are you doing this afternoon? I need to get out of this house or I'm gonna be one of those nutcases. I was thinking about lunch at the Art Museum. Are you free?"

"Sounds cool, but I'm hanging out with Prudence today. The Knights are playing at home. It should be a good game."

"Oh, okay. Well, we'll do something another time."

"No, don't be silly. Why don't you just come with us? We're just going to the football game and then maybe grab something to eat afterward."

"I heard the tickets were sold out."

"No tickets necessary. We'll be in the owner's box. Prudence's mom and dad are gonna be there, too. It's good publicity."

Gia thought a moment. She refused to ask, but even considering the possibility that Keith might also be there gave her a sudden thrill. She might see him again. "I'd love to go, if it's okay with Prudence, of course."

"I'm sure it is. Let me call her, then call you right back."

"Okay, thanks, Val." Gia pressed to disconnect and just sat looking at her view. *Hey, Keith,* she thought, *I'm ready.*

A few minutes later her cell phone rang again. It was Val. Gia picked up. "Hey."

"I just spoke with Prudence. It's no problem. She's gonna pick me up and then we'll stop by and get you. Is an hour too soon?"

"No, not at all. Thanks, I really need this."

"No problem, it'll be fun. We'll see you in about an hour."

Gia didn't waste any time. She locked the balcony door and, having already taken a shower an hour earlier, hurried to her closet to find something to wear. She dressed, pulled her hair back in a bun and then finished getting herself together. Forty-eight minutes later her doorbell rang. She opened it to see Val and Prudence smiling. "Hey," they said in unison.

"Hi, Val. Hi, Prudence," Gia said, hugging and welcoming them into her home. "Thank you so much for letting me tag along today. Come on in, I just have to grab my purse."

"You're perfectly welcome. It's gonna be so much fun," Prudence said. "Have you ever been to a Knights game before?"

"Yes, years ago, before my parents divorced."

"It's so much better and the skyboxes are awesome," Val said.

"I'm really looking forward to it."

"Gia, your home is beautiful and the view of the bridge and the river is breathtaking. I've never been in this building before. I've only seen the view from the opposite side facing the city. My brother used to live right across the street in the building facing this one."

"Really, your brother…"

"Yeah, my brother, Keith," Prudence said as Val smiled. "So, when are you two going to hook up for real?" Prudence added.

Gia's jaw dropped. "I don't know what you're talking about," she said, then looked at Val and frowned.

"Hey, don't look at me. I wasn't the one on the dance floor at the benefit falling in love. That was you and Keith."

"We weren't falling in love. And, Prudence, Keith and I are just business associates."

Prudence smiled. "Well, personally, I think you two would make a great couple. You look good together. And he needs someone in his life that's not all about law and politics. He deserves to be happy and so do you."

"Okay, I'm ready to go." Gia grabbed her purse and they headed out. Prudence drove to the stadium as the three talked about everything from fashion, to music, to celebrities, to foreign policy. When they got to the security gate, Prudence showed her ID and was pointed to an open parking space. They got out and headed up to the skybox.

It was one thing after another for Keith. First the almost fire at City Hall; then one of his clients was facing a flood of bad press and major ethics sanctions because of a tabloid article naming him as the father of his assistant's three-year-old child. The fact that the allegations were true and he'd tried to cover it up didn't help. Then, of course, Lester Jameson had received a major endorsement and seemed to be riding a wave of renewed popularity.

So the last week had been filled with cancelled appointments, constant travel, meetings and the initiation of full damage control on all fronts. All that forced Keith to refocus on what was supposed to be the most important thing in his life—his work. But the problem was all he could think about was Gia. And it made him realize that there was more to his life than work.

But now with most of the fires put out, he took the rare opportunity to sit back and relax with his brothers. It was Sunday afternoon and their brother-in-law was leading the Philadelphia Knights to another victory. The game was tied and Speed had been taking a brutal punishment for the last three quarters plus overtime. But the team's renewed rally was strong and the Knights, led by Michael Speed Hunter, had marched down the field on sheer strength and determination.

Keith handed each of his brothers another nonalcoholic beer, then sat down in front of the huge flatscreen television attached to the wall in his game room. Screened and glassed, heated and cooled, this room was finished and designed for four-season use. This was his sanctuary and his new home away from the craziness of Philly, D.C. and New York. Few came unless specifically invited. They cheered after another near-impossible first-down completion.

The regulation game had already been played. They were now in the last few minutes of overtime. The first to score would win and it was more than obvious that both teams were looking for a victory. "Man, this game is killing me," Drew said as he got up and walked over to the buffet table. It was loaded with every imaginable game-time snack. He grabbed a couple of fried chicken wings and some collard greens and potato salad.

"Yo, bro, bring me back a couple more chicken wings," Jeremy said before taking the last bite of his cheesesteak.

"You want anything, Keith?" Drew asked.

"Nah, I'm good," Keith said, sipping his beer.

Drew walked back over, gave Jeremy a small plate of wings, then took his seat between his two brothers. "I don't know, man. It looks like they just might be able to pull this one off."

Jeremy chuckled. "Hell yeah, Speed is serious about winning this game. Look at him scrambling behind the line. Hey, remind me again why we didn't go to this game?"

"You were supposed to get the tickets and you blew it."

"Oh, yeah, that," Jeremy said, laughing, "my bad."

"I don't know how he does it—football games, practice, national endorsements campaigns and chairman of his nonprofit children's organization, plus a baby on the way in a few months," Keith said.

"Don't forget dealing with Prudence," Drew said. The brothers chuckled. "Seriously, I think she's losing her mind lately. Last week she was trying to hook me up with a model friend she knows in London. I couldn't believe it. She was trying to set me up on a blind date."

"So what happened?" Keith asked.

Drew shook his head, looking more annoyed than he intended. "My date canceled on me at the last minute," he said stiffly. "I gotta admit I was a bit annoyed, but then she texted me and it's all good."

Jeremy and Keith chuckled. "So, who is this model?"

"Her name's Angel Periz."

"I've seen her. She's gorgeous, man."

"Yeah, she is. I saw pictures," Drew said, sounding a little disappointed. "Anyway, I texted her and we've been going back and forth for a while. She's got a wicked sense of humor."

"Sounds like you like her," Keith said.

Drew shrugged noncommittally. "She's funny and smart. I didn't expect that. Anyway, we're gonna hang out the next time she's in the States."

"Prudence playing matchmaker… You know she got that from Mamma Lou," Jeremy said, shaking his head.

"Yeah, but at least Mamma Lou's back on Crescent Island. We're safe until the next time she comes to town."

"So, who was Mamma Lou trying to match?"

"Gia Duncan and Rick Renault," Keith said.

"Now that's a tough match. Can you see those two together?"

"I don't know, they might work," Drew said.

"No, they wouldn't," Keith said in a tone that made both his brothers look at him. "I'm just saying, he doesn't want marriage, we all know that. And she's—"

"Whoa, whoa, check it out," Jeremy said as Speed ran down the sidelines being chased by three huge linebackers. They laughed and cheered as Speed stepped out of bounds. The game clock stopped. The stadium cameras focused on him a few seconds, then cut away to pan the crowd and then focus on the owner's box.

"Man, seriously, when are you gonna get the rest of this place finished?" Jeremy asked. "This could really be a nice place to chill out. Besides, you know I'm not gonna feel like driving back to the city after. If you had more than one bedroom, I could crash here."

"What do you mean? It is done," Keith protested.

Drew laughed. "Dude, a bedroom, a bathroom and a game room isn't what I call done."

"That's all I need for right now, although I'm seriously thinking about getting the kitchen designed in the very near future. I'm getting a little tired of ordering out every time I come here."

"Hey, nothing wrong with ordering out," Jeremy said.

"Jeremy, you need to learn how to cook. You can't order out the rest of your life. Besides—"

"Hey, check it out, there's Mom and Dad in the owner's box," Drew said, interrupting.

Keith focused back on the screen. He knew his parents were going to the game. It was a planned press op, and of course they looked exactly as planned.

"Yo, yo, yo, isn't that your lady, Keith?" Jeremy said, pointing to the television screen.

"Yep, that's Gia Duncan sitting with Prudence and Mom. Who would have guessed?" Drew added.

Keith looked closer to see Gia and his mom with their heads together laughing about something. The sportscasters didn't identify her since the time-out ended and the game began again. "What's she doing there?" he muttered. "And for the record, she's not my lady," Keith also clarified. Drew and Jeremy glanced at each other and smiled knowingly. Keith witnessed the open interaction. "All right, if you've got something to say, say it."

"You know you want her, man. Why don't you just go for it?" Drew said. Keith looked threatening. "I'm just saying."

"Dude, the two of you out on the dance floor at the benefit the other week nearly set the whole floor on fire."

"I have no idea what you're talking about," Keith said innocently.

His brothers laughed. "The way you were looking at her and the way she was looking at you and then that slow-groove dance. I had no idea you had moves like that. Seriously, you had women standing on the sides staring with drool coming out of their mouths."

"Now I know I have no idea what you're talking about."

"Please, don't act like you don't know. Everybody could see that either something was already going on between you or something was about to start."

"It was a dance, that's it. Gia Duncan and I are business professionals. That's all. There's no way we can explore anything else."

"Why not, because of the election?" Jeremy asked.

"That and other factors," he said.

"Man, since when have you let general convention dictate your life? If you want to be with her, tell her."

Keith looked at his brothers and shook his head.

"Ah, come on, man, it's all good. Gia's a nice woman. She's intelligent, gorgeous and her body is perfect. Seriously, I like her and if you don't step up, I just might."

Keith's eyes instantly narrowed. His brothers laughed again. "See, see, that right there. She got you, man. She got you."

"Yeah, she's got me. But right now she doesn't want me."

"Come again?"

"We were moving too fast. She wants to take it slow. That was a week ago."

Jeremy and Drew shook their heads. "And now?" they said.

"And now I'm gonna let her have her time. It's strange, one day I was enjoying my life and the next I can't imagine my life without her." Drew and Jeremy nodded slowly. "You know what, three weeks ago we were worried about Mamma Lou and now look at us."

Jeremy turned back to the television. "Hey, the game's over," he said. Drew and Keith turned to the screen. The game had just ended with the Knights victorious. They watched the replay and highlights and then talked, joked and stayed another hour, helping Keith clean up before heading back to the city. Keith decided to stay until the morning.

Chapter 17

Gia got out of the car after hugging and thanking Val and Prudence for an awesome day. She was still smiling from the last play ending the game. The Knights were on the three-yard line and Speed, knowing he'd take the brunt of the assault with a quarterback sneak, passed the ball and then dived over the unstoppable defensive line as another player ran the football in to score. No one saw it coming. Everyone cheered until the very end. "Thanks so much, I had a blast."

"Anytime. We'll talk to you later," Val said.

"Gia," Prudence called. Gia turned and walked back to the car. "Here, take this. It's Keith's address at his new place. You should stop by and see him. He's there now."

Gia looked at the piece of paper in her hand. "Prudence, really, this isn't necessary. I don't need it."

"We all need somebody sometimes. Just in case. Don't be afraid to go get what you want," she said, then waved as she drove away.

Gia watched them drive off. She shook her head and stuffed the paper in her pocket, then went up to her condo. It was still early and even though she was tired, she was also energized because of the excitement of the day. She freshened up, grabbed a glass of wine and went outside to her balcony and sat down.

She thought about what Prudence had said. *We all need somebody sometimes.* Keith. Being with his parents and his sister all day made her wonder about him. Although no one had mentioned his name, he was right there in her thoughts. She looked around at the surrounding building, wondering which one was his since Prudence hadn't been specific. Then she remembered the piece of paper Prudence had given her. She had said that he was there now. She wondered what he was doing. Gia pulled it out of her jeans pocket and read the address. It was in Chestnut Hill. She didn't know exactly where it was, but she knew the area well.

She went back inside. The solitude of loneliness was all around her. This was her life and it was going to be until she changed it. She started thinking again about what Prudence had said. *Don't be afraid to go get what you want.* Prudence was right and Gia decided to do just that. She grabbed her purse and walked out with one destination in mind. She programmed his address into her GPS and drove listening to the audible directions and the sound of her heart pounding. The closer she got, the faster she drove.

When the GPS announced that she had arrived, she looked up to see a gated stone entranceway. She turned and drove up the driveway to a large three-story stone farmhouse that looked as if it were part of a History Channel remake. It was old, stately and majestic and as far from the twenty-first century as light is from dark. But it was also really beautiful. She looked around. The only vehicle parked out front was a pickup truck. She rechecked the address on the paper and the GPS. This was it.

She got out and walked up to the front door. She was excited and scared and had no idea what she was doing. Just an hour earlier she was at home; now she was standing at Keith's front door. She rang the bell and a few seconds later the door opened. Keith stood in the open doorway obviously stunned to see her.

"Gia," he said quietly.

"Hi," she said, trying not to sound as nervous as she was.

"What are you doing here? How did you…"

"Your sister is very persuasive."

"Prudence, yes, she is. Come on in," he said, stepping aside.

She walked in, hearing the echo of her heels clicking on the polished marble flooring. She looked around. The foyer was huge and completely bare, no furniture and nothing on the walls. Keith closed the door and she turned to him. He looked too good for words. Losing her battle with her desires, she took three steps and wrapped her arms around his neck and kissed him.

This was it—what she'd been wanting for the last week. This was what was missing in her life and this was what she needed now and forever. The kiss instantly swept them away in passion. He wrapped his arms around her waist and pulled her close. Her lips parted and his tongue delved into her mouth. It was the sweetest sensation. Nothing could match this.

She'd been starving and his kiss was the taste of nirvana. Her heart thundered and every nerve ending in her body tingled with the thrill of being in his arms again. She heard a loving moan and realized it came from her. She turned her head. The kiss deepened beyond erotic foreplay as he switched their positions and pressed her against the door, trapping her with his hard body.

He grabbed hold of her butt and picked her up. She wrapped her legs around his body and felt the steel-like hardness of his penis press between her legs. The deep heaviness of his guttural groan told her everything she needed to know. He wanted her as much as she wanted him. Then, from a distance, the sound of joyous laughter resounded. She stopped and looked at him, then pushed to step down, putting distance between them.

Breathlessly, he looked at her, questioning. "What, what?" he said, obviously not having had his fill of her.

"Someone's here. You have company," she said anxiously. It had never occurred to her that he wouldn't be alone. Suddenly, the thought of another woman coming out and seeing them together ran through her mind. She moved away from him, keeping a more respectable distance. "I'm sorry, I should have called." She reached around him for the doorknob.

He covered her hand to stop her. "Gia, don't go. I need—"

"I shouldn't have come. I don't know what I was thinking."

"Keith, man, we're gonna get out of here," Drew said as he walked toward the foyer area. A second later he stopped.

Jeremy was right behind him. "Yeah, we're leaving you with the rest of the cleanup. Oh," he said, stopping right behind Drew.

"Guys, you know Gia Duncan," Keith said, turning to his brothers.

"Yeah, yeah, yes, of course. Hi, Gia. It's good to see you."

"Hi, Gia."

Gia turned around, smiling and feeling like a complete fool. "Drew, Jeremy, hi, it's good to see you again. I'm gonna go."

"No," all three Washington men said at once.

"No, you should stay, really," Jeremy said quickly. "You can keep Keith company while he finishes cleaning up the kitchen."

"Yes, definitely," Drew added, and nodded to Jeremy. "We're gonna head to the side door. Take care, Gia, it was good seeing you. Later, Keith."

Both men turned and quickly headed back the same way they had come. Neither she nor Keith spoke until hearing the sound of a door open and close somewhere in the back of the house.

"I didn't see any cars parked out front," she said.

"They usually park around the back. It's closer to the basketball court and game room, and that's where we usually hang out."

"Oh."

"So, welcome, come on in, have a seat," he said. She looked around the foyer as if to wonder, where? "Oh, right, the house isn't finished yet. I'm doing it room by room. So far I only have three rooms done. We can go to the family room, this way." He led.

"It looks wonderful and beautifully antique-ish. How old is it?" she asked, following him down a side corridor.

"It's old. It was built in 1922. It's hard to imagine what this place looked like then. There's a lot of history in these walls."

They entered the huge family room off the kitchen. She started walking around, looking at everything. It was definitely a man cave. There was a massive television and entertainment center mounted on the wall, comfortable seating, a pool table, slot machines, a poker table to the side, vintage video games and, of course, sports memorabilia everywhere. But it was also cleverly designed and nicely decorated. "This is really cool. You did a great job," she said.

Keith followed her, watching every move she made and admiring the slim fit of her jeans, silk shirt and heels. He stared at her perfect apple bottom and all he could think about was watching her climax on top of him. "Do you have any idea what those jeans are doing to my body right now?"

She glanced over her shoulder, smiling seductively. "No, tell me, what are they doing to your body?" she asked innocently.

"I have a better idea. I'll show you." In three long strides he was standing right behind her. He placed his hands on her shoulders, then eased down her arms and held on to her hips, pulling them back against his crotch. She moaned, feeling their instant connection. He went farther down her body to her butt, then squeezed and massaged firmly. A groan of satisfaction rumbled through his body. "You feel so good."

Gia rolled her head back to lean on his chest and shoulder. His hands came up to her breasts, then went down between her legs and back to her rear again. He licked his lips. "My mouth is so dry. I just want to eat you up."

"Cherries again?" she suggested.

"Nah, I have a much better idea. I've been thinking about it for a while," he whispered right in her ear.

"What is it?" she asked, shivering.

"Later. Turn around." She turned. He scooped

up the hair at the nape of her neck, leaned down to kiss her, but then paused and looked into her eyes. What passed between them in that instant couldn't be spoken. They knew right then that this wasn't just a physical release. This was beyond sex and intimacy. This was love, deep and passionate—the forever kind that came around only once in a lifetime. "I love you," he whispered. She gasped.

The kiss came sweetly followed by a session of tiny erotic nibbles on her lips, eyelids, check, neck and shoulders. Then a split second later he grabbed her rear and picked her up. She encircled his waist with her legs, then wrapped her arms around his neck and everything after that went hazy.

Later, when the deep, lasting, magnificent kiss ended, she was on his lap straddling his hips and he was sitting on the sofa. "So, what other rooms have you completed?" she asked breathlessly.

"The bedroom. Would you like to see it?"

She nodded. "Definitely," she said, then stood up.

"This way," he said, motioning to the staircase in the family room. She walked over and waited for him, then took one step up, and they were at eye level. He licked his lips. "Did I tell you how beautiful you look this evening?"

"Thank you."

"It's the first time I've seen you in jeans. I like them."

"Right back at you," she said, "although I'm not sure I like the shirt."

"Well, we can't have that, can we?" He pulled his

shirt from his jeans and she began unbuttoning it. When it was open she pushed it free and let it rest on the banister. The stunning magnificence of his chest left her speechless. "And, come to think of it, I've never cared much for silk."

"I totally agree," she said, pulling her shirt free as he unbuttoned it. When he finished he helped her take it off, then placed it on top of his shirt. Two perfect mounds faced him.

"If we don't go upstairs to my bed right now, we're gonna make love down here on the pool table."

She glanced behind him and smiled. "Yeah, maybe later."

In an instant he swept her up in his arms. She giggled, then wrapped her hands around his neck and held tight as he carried her upstairs to his bedroom. He walked in, took her to his big four-poster bed, then slowly put her down and stopped. "What, what's wrong?" she asked, seeing the concern on his face.

He shook his head. "I don't have any condoms here."

"I have condoms," she said, smiling, and reached into her back pocket and pulled out two foil packets. Then she reached into the other back pocket and pulled out two more.

"I love the way you think, Ms. Duncan." He sat down and pulled her to stand between his long legs. He slowly traced the full mounds of her breasts with his finger, then dipped between them and unsnapped her bra's front. With the full weight of her breasts freed, he instantly cupped them. She gasped and arched slightly at the feel of his hands on her body again. He leaned in and licked each nipple, sending shivers through her. They hardened instantly.

He unzipped her jeans and eased them down her legs. She kicked off her heels and stepped out of them. He stood and unzipped his jeans and removed everything. He grabbed a condom, then pulled her lace panties down and picked her up again, entering her in one smooth motion. He pressed her back up against the bedpost and began gyrating his hips into her. Each push made her gasp and squeal louder and louder. Then he moved faster and faster.

The steel hardness of his penis hitting her engorged nub sent her reeling. All she could do was hold on until the end. Then one last push and she exploded in shrieks of pure rapture. He laid her down on the bed and continued. This time he was slow and deliberate. He raised her butt higher and put her legs on his shoulders. A few seconds later her body jerked again. Then they came as one.

He rolled to his back, letting her rest. Hours later, just after dark, they went out to a late dinner at a small out-of-the-way café she knew about just off Germantown Pike. They sat in the back, ordered and talked about everything under the sun. As they walked back to the truck, she stopped to go into a small boutique and he walked on to meet her at the truck. Fifteen minutes later she returned with a small shopping bag. He was already waiting in the truck. "What's in the shopping bag?" he asked, recognizing the name on the bag as a women's lingerie boutique.

"It's a gift for you."

"May I see it?" he asked.

"Later," she said.

He smiled, nodding. "Dessert, I'll look forward to it."

They pulled into the driveway and drove around to the back of the house. They got out and headed to the side door. He opened it and she walked in but didn't get far because he pulled her back into his arms, instantly stealing her breath away. He kissed her hard and long, aggressive and demanding. She loved it, a powerful man and an equally powerful kiss. There was nothing timid or maybe about it. It was mind-blowing insanity. Tongues battled and mouths engulfed. Her legs trembled weakly as he pressed her up against the door frame.

This was what she wanted. This was what she needed. Keith had exceptional seductive skills and he applied them earnestly. His hand came up to the nape of her neck to hold her in place as his other hand roamed her body. First, he caressed her breast, and then his hand moved down to her stomach, her waist, her hips and finally, between her legs. She moistened instantly. The thought of having him long, hard and thick inside her made her dizzy.

Then, just as suddenly as it had begun, the kiss slowed and softened to a tender loving embrace. His hands, all over her at first, now caressed and stroked her back and rested tenderly on her rear, pressing her close. When the kiss ended they were both breathless.

"It took all I could do to keep my hands off you at dinner."

"Is that right?" she muttered, reaching down to stroke the length of his hardening penis.

"Oh, you don't play fair," he growled, closing his eyes.

"All's fair in love," she whispered.

He tipped her chin up and looked into her hooded eyes. "Love?" he said softly. She bit at her swollen lips. She knew exactly what he was talking about. The truth was she wanted to say something, but she couldn't. She closed her eyes and shook her head. "I love you." He repeated the words in a quiet hush, carrying on the sweetest whisper, just as he had before.

Her heart paused and she trembled inside. They were just three innocent words. But they went through her like a double-edged blade cutting right to her heart. They had the power to transform a woman who thought she had everything perfectly ordered in her life and didn't need anyone into a woman in love with a man who took her breath away. They were three words that she had longed to hear all her life. She looked up into his promising eyes, feeling the exact same way. "Keith, what if what you feel is just—" she took a tiny breath "—lust?"

He shook his head. "Don't. You can't analyze feelings. It doesn't work like that. They are what they are. Don't be afraid of this."

"Keith, love smothers and chokes and suffocates until there's nothing left to take."

"No, love, real love, lifts up, embraces and gives.

I know what I feel for you, Gia. I can't stop thinking about you and I can't stop wanting to be with you. Lust doesn't keep me up every night since we met. Loving you does. I love you, Gia."

She felt the words penetrate her heart and delve deep into her soul. She knew what she felt for him. This was real. Her heart trembled with the joy of knowing it. Then, without caution, the words slipped out of her mouth before she thought. "I love you, too."

He smiled happily, like a little boy getting exactly what he wanted for Christmas. "Yeah, I like the sound of that. Say it again."

"I love you," she said slightly louder.

He nodded, still smiling. "I love you, too," he said. "Now, one thing you should know about me. It's pretty important. I have never been able to resist eating my dessert first."

Gia laughed, then smiled seductively. "Really?" she said. He nodded assuredly. "I'll tell you what, come upstairs in ten minutes." He nodded. She turned and hurried upstairs with her little shopping bag.

Keith watched her go, then went to the kitchen and opened the refrigerator. He pulled out a bottle of champagne and grabbed two glasses. He checked his cell phone messages and quickly emailed a few replies. Then eight and a half minutes later he walked upstairs As soon as he entered his bedroom, he saw Gia standing beside the bed lighting a candle. His mouth dried instantly. She was leaning over with her back to him. Two perfect cheeks hardened him all over again.

He walked over purposefully and stood right behind her. The hardness of his penis pressed against her. He rubbed each cheek gently, then knelt down and kissed her soft brown skin. "Gia, do you have any idea what you do to me?"

She turned around and posed, dressed in a very skimpy push-up bra and half-panties with lace stitching. "What do you think? Do you like your present?"

He looked down the length of her body and smiled. "Oh, yes." And just like that the beautiful lace outfit was gone in a split second.

He picked her up, took her to the bed, then stripped his clothing off. She sat up, waiting, and then, as soon as he lay down, she got on top and impaled herself. Smiling, she began to move her body up and down, taking him in repeatedly. He held her waist, pulling her breast down to his mouth. She rode him and he suckled her until she exploded and his body shuddered and spasmed, draining his essence into her to the very last drop.

Chapter 18

Late Friday morning Gia sat back in her chair and twirled her pen in her fingers as she sipped her now ice-cold coffee. It didn't really matter how long it had been sitting on her desk because she didn't really taste it anyway. Drinking it was just something to do until it was time to go. She dropped the pen, then picked it up again and tapped it on the desk. She'd gotten in early to work, catching up with several projects. But there was no way she was getting any work done now.

The rest of the office staff had the afternoon off. They had all worked hard all week. When the governor visited the city to endorse the mayor, OCC was right there with questions. The same was true for the mayor's northeast town hall meeting and the citywide electoral debate appearances. For the most part the mayor was respectful and Keith didn't interfere. They easily accommodated OCC and even went out of their way to include them in the economic discussion.

Now the still quietness of the office made her thoughts wander, and Keith was her main focus. It was much more than physical and she knew it. It scared her. But what scared her most was feeling everything she was feeling for him even when they weren't actually together. It was overwhelming. He consumed her thoughts both day and night.

She dropped her pen again and this time it rolled across the desk onto the floor. She scrambled to pick it up just as her open door was pushed wider. She looked up to see Bill march into her office and sit down in the chair across from her. "Lawyers, God save us all from lawyers. We need to talk."

"Actually, I favor lawyers."

"Of course you'd say that," he said snidely.

She looked at him sternly. "Obviously you've forgotten I am a lawyer."

He looked at her dismissively. "That's right, you are."

"What's up, Bill, what do we need to talk about?"

"The election is getting close and we need to announce an endorsement backing a mayoral candidate."

"Not necessarily."

"We're a community organization. People listen to us. We have power. They need to know what we think. So, listen, I've been checking out both candidates and I think we have a real good chance of forwarding the OCC agenda if we back Lester Jameson."

Gia laughed. "Are you kidding me? No way. Absolutely not. The man is an egomaniacal fraud, plus he's being investigated."

"That's all bogus, drummed-up campaign rhetoric," Bill said.

"Sounds pretty legit to me," Gia said, "and why does Jameson think he's getting OCC's endorsement? Did you promise it?"

"See, I knew it. You're being brainwashed by all those political commercials. Don't believe the hype. Blake has been going negative since the beginning of this campaign."

"What are you talking about, Bill?"

"At least I have an open mind. You apparently don't."

"My objection to Jameson has nothing to do with the mayor and everything to do with Councilman Jameson's character, or lack thereof."

The defensive rant started and continued for the next several minutes. Getting more and more excited, Bill recited every Jameson talking point, including the mayor's apparent inability to work with the current city council, the high unemployment rate, the increase in crime and the fact that only four of the noted unions in the city had backed him. After that Gia stopped listening.

"…and then I hear that Sam Duncan comes into the office and nobody even thinks to tell me."

Hearing her father's name, Gia looked up. Bill was staring at her. "Bill, he came to see me about a personal matter. He is my father and his visit had nothing to do with OCC."

"Everything going on in this office has to do with OCC," he said. She chuckled. "Oh, you think that's funny?" he snapped.

"Bill, chill out, what is wrong with you?" she asked.

"I don't see how you can be this nonchalant. This place is falling apart. The volunteers are deserting us for cash-paying jobs with politicians and in a few weeks we're gonna be left holding nothing but our—"

"Bill. Seriously, what is wrong with you?"

"Me? You. What the hell is going on? I read in Danny's blog this morning that you attended the Knights Ball last Saturday evening and hung out with the Washington family. So, what's going on? Is OCC getting in bed with the mayor now?"

Gia immediately took umbrage. "I am not getting into bed with the mayor. And you need to rein your friend in. He's tearing this office apart with his insinuations and lies."

"How far from the truth is he? What the hell is going on, Gia? Are we in this together or not?"

"First of all, I didn't hang out with the Washington family at the Knights Ball. I was there with a friend and they were also there. Yes, I ran into them. My friend Val is friends with them. We spoke. We talked. And yes, Keith Washington and I danced. But that's all you need to know."

"I'm not so sure that's all there is. You were dancing with him. What's going on between you two?"

"What I do in my personal life is none of your business."

"It is when and if it affects this office. Now, if you're playing him to get funding or inside information, fine, that's one thing, but if he's playing you—"

"Nobody's playing anybody. Why does it have to be about politics? Why can't it just be about two people meeting and talking? We talked. He told me about the plan he and the mayor are putting together."

"What plan?" Bill asked.

"The mayor's economic plan," she said.

"Tell me about it."

Gia laid out exactly what Keith had told her Saturday night at the diner. Bill nodded and asked a few questions as he listened intently. He was surprised; it was really pretty good. With some hard work and a lot of fortitude, he agreed, his economical plan could really work. Of course, he felt there could be a few improvements, but overall it was a very good workable base.

"And Keith Washington told you all this," he clarified. She nodded. "Why?"

"Why? Because he and the mayor are actually trying to turn this city's economics around," she said. "This economical plan is good. It could work."

"Perhaps," Bill said, shrugging.

"If you're done, I'm gonna go visit my grand-mother."

"Fine, go, I have an appointment I need to get to anyway."

"Are you gonna meet me at Keith's office?"

"Yeah, yeah, I'll be there," he said, already out the door.

Gia gathered her things and walked out into the lobby area. Bill was already gone, so she locked up and headed for her car.

The decision was easier than he'd thought.

Bill strolled into Lester Jameson's office smiling as if he'd just swallowed the Cheshire Cat. He had a caveat and he knew that if he played his cards right, this small piece of information could be par-leyed into a new career. He thought about what he was doing and what Gia and Julia would think after-ward. He shook his head. It didn't really matter—as far as he was concerned, it was every man for him-self at this point.

Julia had overlooked him and chosen her grand-daughter to run OCC. Fine. And now her grand-daughter was playing with Keith Washington. That was fine, too. He wasn't culpable. But there was no reason why he couldn't get his payday out of all this. But really, all this was a moot point. This was a new world of instant information. And whoever con-trolled the flow of information controlled the world. He knew that. Keith knew that. OCC was irrelevant at this point. It was bloggers and spin doctors that made the money, shaped the politicians and affected a political race.

Lester Jameson was falling in the polls like an anvil out of a hot-air balloon. He had had a chance once, but now he was a pitiful man trying desperately to hold on to the last bits of his political integrity and his last shred of dignity. The news media had dug deep into his background and come up with a number of questionable actions, and now he was hemorrhaging money and political backing. But with his help his campaign could be revived. One innocent piece of information placed strategically in the right hands could turn this election around.

Danny had it right, but all that writing and blogging was too tedious. And there was no way he was going to be begging for money all of his life. He'd learned his lesson. It was time to step up and take his place among the power elite. It was time to seriously get paid.

Lester opened his office door, smiling. "Bill, come on in. Have a drink. It's good to see you again. It's been too long."

Bill stood and nodded. "It's good to see you, too, Councilman. Thank you for seeing me on such short notice."

"Not at all." Lester smiled with wide yellowing teeth. "It's always good to have OCC in the office."

"Actually better than you think."

"Sounds interesting. What do you have for me?"

"I've got good news and bad news. The bad news

is that it's pretty evident that the mayor will not be backing your economic plan. He's all set to veto it."

Lester nodded. "Yeah, I expected as much. But it's a good plan and it will work for the city. But all that's fine, too. Everyone will see it for exactly what it is, a campaign snub. Ultimately it'll only make him look petty and narrow-minded to turn it down."

"Perhaps, but what if I told you the head of OCC and the mayor's son were romantically involved?"

"I wouldn't be surprised," Lester said. "Tell me more."

"And what if I told you I know the mayor's economic plan?"

The corner of Lester's lips tipped up slowly. He obviously liked what he was hearing.

Bill smiled, knowing that this was it, the beginning of his new career.

Chapter 19

Gia drove to the nursing home and went directly to the solarium. She knew at this time of day it was her grandmother's favorite place to be. She walked in and looked around, not seeing her grandmother anywhere. Since she knew her grandmother didn't have any tests scheduled and it was too late for her morning therapy, she couldn't imagine where she'd be. She went upstairs and stopped at the nurse's station. "Excuse me, my grandmother, Julia Banks, wasn't downstairs in the solarium."

"No, she has company in her apartment."

"Oh, okay, thanks." Gia headed to her grandmother's room. She knocked but didn't get an answer. She opened the door and stepped inside, then stopped cold. She saw her grandmother laughing and smiling happily. She had guests. Mamma Lou was with her and another woman whom she hadn't seen in almost six years. It was her grandmother Loretta Duncan. Gia walked over slowly. "Hi," she barely croaked out. Three pairs of loving eyes turned to her.

"Ladies, look who's here. Perfect timing, another wonderful surprise," Julia said.

"Mamma Lou, Grandma Loretta, what are you doing here?"

"Visiting with two very dear friends," Louise said.

"Hello, Gianna," Loretta said.

"I don't understand, Grandmom, you and Grandma Loretta are talking, but how? I thought…"

Julia smiled and took Gia's hand. "Sweetheart, I should've learned a long time ago that holding on to a grudge never changed anything for the better. It only makes you work harder to be angry."

Gia looked at her other grandmother. "It's good to see you, Grandma Loretta."

Loretta stood and opened her arms. Gia went to her and they hugged warmly. Louise and Julia looked on happily. "I don't understand. How did you know…"

"I called Louise. She brought me here to see Julia and I'm so happy she did. It was time to let go of old pain."

"What about Granddad?" Gia asked.

"Oh, baby," Loretta said, touching Gia's cheek softly, "your grandfather is stubborn and determined to get his way and I love him dearly. It doesn't mean I don't see his flaws."

"Did he really dislike my mother so much?"

"The moment he met your mother he knew your father would never be the same man. Her love changed him. Then, when she died, your father was devastated. Your grandfather thought that the only way he could secure the family's future was to keep you with the family by any means necessary."

"That's why he lied about Grandmom?"

She nodded. "He was trying to protect you."

"Protect me or his money, his future?"

"Both. He knew you were his future and he needed you to be strong."

"I am strong, just not like him."

"He knows that and he is very proud of you and one day he'll tell you so."

"Gia, come sit, join us. It's tea time," Julia said.

Gia sat down happily. She still couldn't believe what she was seeing. This was truly a remarkable sight. The three women she adored the most in her life had come together.

They were sitting at a table with several tiered trays of finger sandwiches, biscuits, scones and dishes of cream, jams and lemon curd. There was a small side table with several pots of tea, cups and saucers and delectable desserts. Tea was being poured by the caterer, compliments of Louise and her grandmother. Gia joined them. High tea was a fantastic idea. The crazy day had turned completely around.

A few minutes later they were sipping tea, eating delicacies, talking and laughing about fond memories. Then the conversation changed. "So, Gianna, tell me, is there a special someone in your life right now?" her grandmother asked.

"I'm hanging out with someone."

"Is that some kind of code?" Louise asked. Everyone laughed. Gia glanced at Louise, knowing she really wanted her to be with Rick Renault.

"Mamma Lou, I know you're a matchmaker, but right now I'm very happy. Yes, there is someone and he makes me very happy and he's a really good guy."

"Whoever he is, he's a very lucky man," her grandmother said.

"And I'm a very lucky woman," Gia said.

"Sweetheart, that's all we have ever wanted for you. Be happy and be loved," her grandmother said. Louise and Loretta agreed.

"I am very happy."

A half hour later she was kissing each woman and saying goodbye. As soon as she as she got in her car, she was overflowing with love. Seeing both grandmothers and Mamma Lou was overwhelming and now she was headed to see Keith. The day had definitely gotten better.

She got to Keith's office and parked in the same spot as before. She got out, headed to the elevator and arrived at the Washington & Associates Law Firm at exactly 2:52. Bill was nowhere in sight. She called and texted him but didn't get an answer or reply. If Bill didn't show up she'd be in Keith's office alone—again. Just the thought sent shivers through her body. She smiled and bit at her lower lip. Good Lord, her body was already starting to get wet just thinking about him and...

"Ms. Duncan." Gia looked up like a kid getting caught drawing on the wall. "Keith is ready for you. This way please."

She stood, took a deep breath, straightened her skirt and followed. Halfway down the hall she heard her name and turned.

"Gia, hey, I'm here," Bill said, hurrying to follow Gia down the law office corridor. "Damn, look at this place. Is it a law office or the friggin' west wing of the White House? Did you check out the lobby? I mean, damn, what's up with that waterfall and atrium?"

"Yes, I've seen it," Gia said tightly, knowing something was wrong with Bill.

"I wonder how much those two paintings cost out there. I swear I saw them in the museum last year and they don't look like fakes. This place is loaded."

"No, you are," Gia hissed. He smelled of liquor even though he'd professed to be on the wagon for the last two years. "Bill, please tell me you haven't been drinking today of all days."

"I'm celebrating and I'm not drunk if that's what you're asking me."

"Celebrating what?" she asked.

"The beginning of a new day," he said cryptically.

Gia shook her head, exasperated. This had potential to be totally embarrassing, and right now this was the last thing she needed.

"You're late. We were supposed to meet and talk before the meeting. What happened?"

Bill smiled happily. "Yeah, well, it is what it is.

I had some phone calls to make and business to attend to."

"Fine, let's just get this done." As soon as Gia walked into Keith's office, the memories flooded back to her. They had made love against his desk, on his desk, on the sofa and on the conference table, then again on the sofa. But there was no sign of anything. It was the same office, but it was pristine.

"Damn, look at this office," Bill said. "Now, this is the kind of office I need at OCC. It immediately shows power and prestige. I can seriously see myself sitting at that desk. Check it out."

He walked over. Gia's heart jumped.

"Good afternoon," Keith said, walking into his office. His assistant, Kate, followed. "Can we get either of you anything before we get started? Water, tea, coffee?"

"Yeah, I'll have a double cappuccino," Bill ordered.

"Nothing, I'm fine," Gia said, hearing the tenseness in her voice.

"Are you sure?" Keith asked.

"Yes, positive."

Keith looked at Kate. She nodded, knowing to just get Bill's coffee. "How was the traffic getting here? It can get crazy this time of day."

"We didn't come here to talk about the traffic," Bill began.

"Bill," Gia warned.

"What? Hey, I'm sure Keith here knows exactly what I'm talking about. Our time is just as valuable as his. Am I right?"

"You're absolutely right, Bill. Please have a seat. We'll get started." He motioned for them to sit at the conference table. The conference table where he had licked and sucked cherry juice off her naked body. Gia didn't move. It wasn't until Bill sat down and turned to her that she timidly walked over. Gia sat as far away as she could from the spot where Keith had licked and enjoyed her body.

"So, Keith," Bill began casually, "I hear the mayor's leaning toward vetoing the economic and jobs bill going through the city council. Why would he do something like that? Wouldn't that be considered political suicide?"

"I'm not privy to the mayor's thought process, so I have no idea what he will or won't do with the council chairman's plan."

"Have you read it?" Bill asked.

"Yes."

"What do you think?" Bill asked.

"In my opinion it's lacking. The plan could be a lot better. It gives away too much power to corporations and those who answer to shareholders and not the citizens of this city."

"But you do approve of the general concept," Bill said.

"No."

"I think you're being shortsighted on this issue. We've been working with Chairman Jameson and he has the answer."

"Respectfully, he doesn't even know the question," Keith said.

"Keith, Bill, I think we need to get back on track.

We're here to discuss ways of opening communication between the mayor's office and OCC. Now, you told me that the mayor was interested in working more closely with us. I'm all for that and I'm sure Bill is also interested in hearing how we can make this work."

Keith turned and smiled at her. "I doubt Bill is very interested in that, are you, Bill?"

Kate walked in with Bill's coffee. For a few moments Bill was busily engrossed with the drink. She glanced at Keith. He had already been staring at her. He smiled again. She quickly looked away.

"Shall we begin?" Keith said as he opened and pressed a key on his laptop. The screen inset within the conference room table instantly changed to the same document he had on his screen. "If you'll look at the mayor's interaction programs, you'll see that he's already connected with a number of community organizations. In monthly meetings he and his team have had remarkable success in getting programs to the people most affected and in need."

He pressed a few keys, highlighting several major corporations that would be partnering with the city's new economic plans and how they would factor into the community assistance programs. "These companies and corporations have been instrumental in the mayor's community outreach programs. With these models already in the works and through the new economic plan, we have approached a number of interested partners to propose—"

"What other corporations?" Bill asked.

"The mayor will be highlighting them as soon as—"

"Yeah, yeah, yeah, I know, but who are they?" he repeated.

Keith smiled. "That's not gonna happen, Bill. You're gonna have to wait until the mayor is ready to release their names and his plan."

"See, this is why OCC is leaning toward endorsing Lester Jameson," Bill said. Gia's eyes instantly widened and her jaw dropped as she looked at Bill, then at Keith. "Your mayor has never really done anything except line his pockets."

"Bill—" Gia began.

"Respectfully, Bill, I believe you have Mayor Washington confused with his opponent, Lester Jameson, and the previous administration. That said, perhaps we should—"

Kate knocked and walked in. She looked at Keith and nodded. Keith stood. "Excuse me, I'll be right back."

He walked out of the room, leaving an intoxicating scent of musk and spice in his wake. God, she loved that cologne even though she had no idea what it was. She remembered the first time she smelled it. He was standing right behind her at the community center. Then she inhaled it the second time and again he was standing right behind her, right here in this office, and his hands were rocking her world.

Bill got up and walked over to Keith's chair. He sat down and began flipping through the screens.

"What are you doing?" she whispered.

"Cutting this meeting short."

"Are you insane? What was that about OCC endorsing Lester Jameson? I never agreed to anything like that. I have no intention of backing Jameson."

"It's business. We need Jameson and we have to play this smart."

"Bill, I don't know what's got into you, but I'm not playing this macho game."

"But you'll play it with him."

"What?" Gia said, quickly thinking he knew about them.

"Yeah, I know everything."

"Everything what? There's nothing to know," she bluffed.

"I know he's just using you to get the OCC endorsement."

"What?"

"He'll do anything to help his father. You told me that he's incredibly loyal, right? So now all of a sudden you think he's in love with you." Bill shook his head with pity. "He's using you, girl."

"Bill, this is a business meeting, not a date."

"You could have fooled me."

"Meaning?"

"You're looking at him like he's the last piece of meat in a buffet dinner filled with cannibals. All he has to do is look in your face and snap his finger and you'd lie down right here on this table."

Gia's stomach jumped. "I can't believe you just said that."

"The only thing saving us is the fact that he doesn't know you exist other than to get what he wants. And I'm not saying this to be mean, I'm saying it because if he ever looks in your eyes he'd know that all he needs to do is sleep with you and he'd have the endorsement."

Gia was speechless. Just then, Keith came back into the room. "I'm sorry, there's been a situation and I have to reschedule this meeting."

"Is there a problem?" Gia asked, seeing the strained concern in Keith's eyes.

Bill stood. "Yeah, sure, just give us a call. You cancelled our meeting last week, what's one more cancelled meeting with OCC."

"As with last week, this is unavoidable. Thank you for understanding." Keith shook Bill's hand and gave him a business card. Then he turned to Gia. She was still seated. He held out a card to her. She took it slowly, then stood. "I'll have my assistant call and set up another meeting."

"Before the election on Tuesday, of course. That way you might just get our endorsement," Bill said smugly. "That gives you exactly three days." Then he downed the rest of his cappuccino.

Keith exhaled with obvious exasperation. "Bill, I understand your caution, but this isn't about getting an endorsement. This is about helping a community and rebuilding a city's trust. Yes, having the OCC's endorsement would be great. It would be icing on the cake. But the mayor will win this election without it. Now, if you'll excuse me." He walked out.

"What an idiot," Gia muttered as soon as Keith left the room.

"See, that's what I'm talking 'bout. Now you're on my side again, the right side."

"Not him, *you*," Gia snapped at him, then walked out.

Bill looked around the empty office; then, seeing his cup and saucer, he grabbed them from the conference room table and stuffed them in his jacket pocket. He turned to see Keith's assistant standing at the open door. Kate smiled, seeing exactly what he did. "This way out, Mr. Axelby."

Bill dropped the cup and saucer on the table and strolled out. "Yeah, whatever," he said, catching up with Gia at the elevators.

"Are you going back to the office?" she asked him.

"No, I'm gonna make a stop. It's time to make a move."

She wasn't interested in his cryptic meaning, so she just let his comment go. Whatever he had to do was fine with her. She didn't want to deal with him right now. "All right, whatever, I'll see you later."

As soon as Gia got to her car, she pulled out her cell phone and texted Keith.

I had no idea Bill was going to go off like that. I still hope we can get together and talk. I'm very encouraged by your ideas. She waited a few minutes, but got no reply.

Chapter 20

The message from his father's campaign office was simple. Lester Jameson was doing a press conference in thirty minutes. Keith hated to cut his time short with Gia, but he had no choice. He had always felt that law and business would always be his top priority, but now he had a new priority—his love for Gia. He smiled, thinking that she looked incredible. Just seeing her, even briefly, had changed his demeanor.

His cell phone beeped. It was a message from Gia. He smiled and was typing a reply when a phone call from his father interrupted him. He answered the call. "Hey Dad, what's up?"

"Where are you?"

"I'm still at the office. I'm headed your way now."

"Turn on channel seven news now," Blake said.

"Okay, give me a second." Keith dropped his briefcase onto the chair and grabbed the remote control and turned on the large-screen TV in his office. He switched to channel seven to see Lester Jameson standing in his City Hall office with two OCC members at his side.

"What the hell?" Keith increased the volume.

"…as allegations have been brought to my attention from local blogger Danny Mead and OCC head, Bill Axelby. Should these allegations prove true and viable, then it puts the mayor's actions in question and we need to look very seriously at the power given to our elected officials. No one, I repeat, no one is above the law in this city, and I promise right now to see that this investigation is handled fairly and thoroughly and lasts as long as needed. And that said, I'd like to…"

"What was that?" Keith asked aloud.

"That's what I want to know," Blake said, still on the phone.

"I'm on my way," Keith said, in full damage control mode. He made phone calls from his car, setting a response in motion. If Lester wanted to fight dirty to the end, then he was ready.

Twenty minutes later Keith parted a throng of reporters still camped out at City Hall. By the time he'd gotten to his father's office, he was furious. It was no mistake. He stood in the office watching the news feed again with his mother and father. The replay was exactly the same as it had been a half hour earlier. Bill Axelby stood beside Lester Jameson as the announcement was made. He smiled and nodded as Lester spoke about integrity and the future of the city.

"What happened?" Marian asked Keith.

"I don't know yet," Keith said, shaking his head, "but I intend to find out."

"How is OCC involved?" Blake asked.

"I told Gia the general economic plan and it looks like she went to Jameson with it," Keith said in utter surprise.

"Disappointing," Blake said.

"Yes, very," Marian agreed.

Keith's eyes narrowed. He fumed as he watched Bill formally announce the OCC position in endorsing Lester. The fact that he and Gia had just been in his office an hour earlier made it worse. "I'll find out what happened."

"No, let it go. The OCC endorsement is lost. We'll move on."

Keith knew in his heart that it wasn't that easy. There was no way he was just going to move on that easily. Gia had betrayed and used him and he needed to know why.

There was a knock on the office door. Drew, Jeremy, Prudence and Michael walked in. Megan followed and nodded to Keith.

"Dad, you have a press conference in thirty minutes. We're all set. Are you ready?"

Blake nodded. Marian stepped to his side and kissed him tenderly. Their sons and daughter smiled, warmed by the embrace. This was what the Washington family did better than anyone. They stood together no matter what.

Gia drove back to the office and hurried inside on hearing the phone ringing. As soon as she got to Bonnie's desk, she saw that all six lines were lit up and ringing. She knew instantly that something was going on. She pressed the buttons silencing and putting on hold all the phones. Then she hurried to her office and turned on the television. Lester Jameson was being interviewed.

"...if these allegations are true, then we need to look very seriously at the power given our elected officials. No one, I repeat, no one is above the law in this city, and I promise right now to see that this investigation is handled fairly and thoroughly and lasts as long as needed. And that said, I'd like to..."

"What allegations?" she muttered as her cell phone rang, assuming this was what prompted Keith to end their meeting so abruptly. She looked at the caller ID. It was Val. She answered just as a commercial came on. She turned the volume down. "Hey, Val, what's up?"

"Hey, hi, how are you?" she said awkwardly. "I know you have your hands full right now. I just wanted to make sure you were okay and let you know that I'm here if you want to talk. Did you hear from Keith yet?"

"No, why? What do you mean, about what happened today? Did he say something to you?"

"Gia, it's on the news," Val said.

Gia looked back at the television screen.

"...allegedly this is only the beginning in the latest scandal coming out of City Hall..."

"Val, let me call you back."

"Okay, whatever time, it doesn't matter. Call me."

Gia ended the call and turned up the television's volume. The camera cut back to the news anchor at the desk.

"Again, our top story, allegations of bribery, intimidation and corruption in Mayor Washington's office. More after these commercial messages."

"What?" Gia flipped channels twice, looking for the full story. Then she waited impatiently. A few minutes later the anchor came back. She turned the volume up and waited for the full story. The report stunned her:

"This evening's top story, Lester Jameson has initiated a panel to look into the mayor's fraudulent actions regarding corruption and kickbacks, citing deals made with large corporations for personal gain in the guise of an economic recovery program. Also, this breaking report, OCC, the Organization for Community Change, the group responsible for these allegations, has endorsed Councilman Chairman Lester Jameson for mayor of Philadelphia."

"What? Oh, my God, Bill, what have you done?" she said, looking at her cell phone. Keith hadn't returned her text messages and he hadn't called. She sent another text.

Keith, please call me, doesn't matter how late.

A second later her phone rang. She answered, expecting to hear Keith's voice. It wasn't him. It was her grandmother. "Hi, Grandmom," she said. "I can't talk right now. I'm—"

"Yes, I just saw the news report. What's going on over there?" Julia asked.

"Bill endorsed Lester Jameson without telling me. I think they've been talking about this and planning it for a while. I never thought he'd jump ship like this."

"I presumed as much. He always wanted more than OCC could give him. Perhaps he'll find what he needs with Lester. But that doesn't matter now. What's your move?"

"Keith probably thinks I betrayed him. I called him and left messages, but he hasn't returned my calls."

"Don't worry about Keith right now."

"Grandmom, you don't understand. Keith and I—"

"I know, sweetheart. You're in love with him."

"Yes, I am," Gia softly admitted.

"I'm so happy for you, but you'll talk to him later and explain. He'll understand that Bill acted on his own."

"I hope so. But right now I need to get control of OCC. I'm gonna make an announcement tomorrow morning that Bill was solely representing himself in his decision to endorse Jameson and I'll disavow everything."

"That's a good start, but it wouldn't completely restore faith."

"I know, but it'll help. OCC will be endorsing the mayor."

"Good," Julia said, "I'm very glad to hear that."

"Too late for that, it's already done."

Gia turned around, hearing the comment. She saw Bill standing in her office doorway. He was smiling and holding a bottle of champagne.

"Grandmom, I'll call you right back," she said, disconnecting. "Are you insane? What have you done?" Gia said as she looked at Bill coldly.

"I did what you should have. I made a decision based on facts and not on my hormones. Man, you should see the party at Jameson's headquarters. Now, they know how to celebrate—champagne, not beer and cold pizza."

Bonnie and Linda hurried into the office. "Hey," Bonnie said, out of breath, "I saw the news tonight. I didn't know OCC was gonna make an endorsement announcement. I don't have a press release ready. What do you want me to write? The phones are already ringing off the hook. They're probably looking for a follow-up announcement from you, Gia."

"I'll tell you what to write," Bill said. "I have some notes and highlights I want to stress. OCC will be—"

"Gia, what do you want me to write?" Bonnie said.

"OCC does not endorse Lester Jameson. I personally don't endorse Lester Jameson. Bill, you can endorse anyone you choose but you do not represent OCC."

"The only reason you want to endorse Washington is that you're sleeping with his son."

Bonnie's and Linda's jaws dropped as they turned in her direction for a response.

"What I do in my personal life and my relationships is none of your business."

"They are when they affect this office."

Gia smiled, shaking her head. "You are a piece of work. All this just to, what, to get in good with Jameson? What did he promise you, money, fame? Do you really think he's gonna deliver?"

"It's true, isn't it?"

"Get out!" she demanded.

"Gladly," Bill said, handing Bonnie the empty bottle of champagne as he walked out.

Gia took a deep breath and looked at Bonnie and Linda still standing in the office doorway. "Are you ladies still with me, with OCC?"

"Yeah, we're here with you."

"Thanks, we have a lot of work to do." Gia looked at her watch. It was seven-thirty. "We need to make an announcement for the eleven o'clock news. Let's get busy."

The first thing Gia did was send a text message.

Bill went rogue.

Again, there was no reply from Keith, so the next few hours she was on full damage control. She'd been trying to put out media fires all evening. Bill was constantly on the news. She sent out a press release, a blog, made phone calls to the media answering questions and updated all OCC social networks. She did everything. But it was obvious that she needed to do more. Bill had always acted as the face of OCC. But she knew it was time for her to take center stage and step in front of the camera and speak.

She called Val. "Hey, I know it's late, but do you think your friend Whitney Abbott at WPVI Action News TV Station will give me a fair interview?"

"I know she will. She'd love to have you on. Let me call her."

Gia hung up and waited all of five minutes. Val called back. "Whitney cleared the first segment of her morning talk show, but she wanted to know if you were up to going live tonight."

"Yes, I am," Gia said.

With that response it happened just that fast. Before she knew it, plans and arrangements had been made and the network was sending Whitney down to the OCC office for an exclusive. Thankfully Val and Prudence came with her, adding moral support.

"Don't worry, Gia, you'll be fine," Whitney said. "I'll ask you a few simple questions to get you started. Just answer the questions as honestly as you can and then you just tell us what you want us to know."

Prudence smiled. "You're a natural, you're gonna do great."

Gia looked at Val, getting two thumbs up. "You got this."

Gia nodded and smiled. Whitney asked her if she was ready. She nodded again and then Whitney's cameraman started a countdown with his fingers. He got to number two, then pointed to Whitney. They were on.

She was honest and endearing and the camera loved her. She answered Whitney's questions and ended with OCC's firm endorsement for Blake Washington.

Shortly afterward she got the text message she'd been waiting for.

Keith: Late dinner?

Gia: YES!

Chapter 21

At one thirty Saturday morning Gia drove to Keith's home in Chestnut Hill. It was dark but the houselights were on and she knew he was waiting for her. She got out of her car and walked to the front door guided by the landscape lighting along the path. Keith opened the door before she got there. It looked as if he had just gotten in also. He stood smiling and holding his hand out to her.

Gia smiled, knowing this was what she needed, to see him. She took his hand and he pulled her into his welcoming embrace. She closed her eyes and melted into his arms. She never wanted to leave and never wanted this feeling to end. "Thank you," she whispered. "Seeing you makes everything so right."

"You're welcome." He kissed her and she wrapped

her arms around his neck. She'd never felt so loved in her life. This was what she always wanted.

"Thank you for endorsing my father."

"You're welcome. It was deserved."

"Come in."

She walked in and turned to him. "That's the first time you referred to him as your father. You usually call him the mayor." He nodded. "We need to talk."

"We will, later. Come."

She followed him, but instead of going to the family room, they went up to his bedroom. As soon as he opened the door she was overwhelmed by the romantic beauty. The room was softly lit by candles aglow on the fireplace mantel and a welcoming blaze in the fireplace. "This is so beautiful."

"A gift for you." He handed her a small shopping bag. She recognized the logo. It was from the same boutique as before.

She smiled. "Don't you mean for you?"

He smiled as he popped a champagne cork. "Oh, yeah, it's definitely for me."

She laughed as he handed her a filled glass. "Are we celebrating?"

"Yes, we're celebrating you. Freedom—you made OCC yours."

They toasted and then she took a sip and sighed happily. "Keith, I need you to know that I had nothing to do with what happened. I would never betray your trust. I did tell Bill about your father's program and the companies, but I had no idea he was—"

"Don't worry about it. It's done and everything's fine."

She nodded, knowing that it was the truth. Shortly after her on-air interview, information had begun coming to light about Danny and Bill's involvement with Lester's campaign. It was far more involved than she thought with promises made and money exchanged. She suspected Keith knew all along.

Then video of Danny's screaming rant outside at the press conference was shown. As the author of the allegations against the mayor, both his blog and character had quickly begun to suffer. Then his soon-to-be ex-wife stepped up and nailed him with spousal abuse and delinquent child support payments. Lester denied knowing anything and completely turned on both men as they all blamed OCC. But with her recent on-air interview, their finger-pointing accusations lacked validity.

"Are you hungry?" he asked, walking to the table and uncovering the dishes. "I stopped by the diner and picked up some—"

She came up behind him and started pulling his shirt free from his pants. "Like you said downstairs, later." He turned around and she kissed him as their passions ignited. He undressed her and she undressed him. Then, standing naked in the glow of the fireplace, they kissed and touched, embracing the sensual feel of their bodies. Their erotic shadows, first two, then one, merged into a sensual dance displayed on the wall.

But foreplay was taking too long. He took her

hand and led her to the big four-poster bed. She lay back, waiting as he covered himself. Then he entered her in one smooth, easy motion and they made sweet, slow sensual love while gazing into each other's eyes.

Hours later, with the bed rumpled and the covers tossed to the side, Keith and Gia lay in each other's arms. "I can't believe it. Time moved too quickly. I feel like I just got here," she muttered. He hummed his agreement. She sighed. "I've got to leave soon. It's almost dawn."

He wrapped his arms around her tighter. "Or not," he said.

"It's Saturday morning, the day after craziness, time to get back to reality. I have to go to work. You have to go to work."

"Or not," he muttered again. "You could stay," he added.

"Can't, I have nothing to wear."

"That's a good idea. I'm totally okay with that."

"Okay with what?" she asked.

"You wearing nothing." He grinned, chuckling.

"You are a dirty old man, Keith Washington," she said, then leaned up to see him smiling with his eyes still closed. They both laughed softy. "I guess I could put on whatever's in that small shopping bag, but I have a feeling we wouldn't be getting a lot of work done."

"You've got that right," he assured her.

"Actually, since the staff stayed late last night, I gave everyone the morning off."

"What about you?" he asked.

"I planned on working from home this morning."

"Good idea, we can both work here this morning."

"Stop tempting me," she said. "Besides, I can't even imagine you working from home."

"I have in the past on occasion, but not often. So let's do it. We'll work from here this morning—afterward."

"What do you mean afterward?" she questioned, then giggled as he rolled on top of her and pulled the covers over them. They made love again with slow, sensual and deliberate ease. Then, just as dawn approached, they fell asleep.

Two hours later they ate breakfast and sat comfortably in his family room working. Gia, dressed in Keith's baggy sweats and a T-shirt while her clothes were in the washer and dryer, made phone calls to shore up OCC's position. Keith stayed on the phone with his father and assistants most of the morning.

With identical laptops opened across from each other, she worked on one side of the large desk and he across from her on the other side. Every once in a while she would look up to see him gazing at her from over the top of his monitor. "Get back to work, Keith Washington," she scolded like a schoolteacher.

He smiled. "Or what?" he challenged.

"Or no dessert before dinner," she warned.

"Yes, ma'am." He buried his head and began typing faster and faster. She laughed and he joined in. "You know, I could definitely get used to this."

"Used to what, working from home?" she asked.

"No, waking up with you, being with you all night and day."

"Is that right?" she continued his joke.

"Oh, yeah."

"Okay, sounds good, although I couldn't just move in. That would be morally wrong. You'd have to make an honest woman of me. Are you prepared to do that, Mr. Washington?" she joked.

"Yeah, I can do that," he said very seriously.

Her heart slammed hard. The look in his eyes stilled her. He was serious and they both knew it. Still, she chuckled nervously. "Okay, you do that, but right now, focus, get yourself back to work."

Gia quickly buried her head and began typing, but she had no idea what she was working on or why. She just busied her hands to stop them from shaking. And she dared not look up no matter how much she wanted to.

Then she heard him begin typing and felt safe to glance up. She did, quickly, seeing him back to work as she had instructed. She took a deep breath. Thankfully the moment was over. Against all odds and the mental storm raging in her head, she got some work done. Then, just before noon, they stopped for lunch. She changed her clothes back to what she had worn the day before, grabbed her laptop and followed him to a small restaurant nearby. They ate and enjoyed the last few minutes of togetherness. Then, after lunch, they parted and promised to get together later that evening.

As soon as Gia got to her office, she felt safe

again. But all she could think about was Keith and that one moment. Was he serious? Did they just agree to marry? She shook her head, still trying to figure out what had happened. Then it hit her. What if he was serious—

She opened her laptop and instantly realized her mistake. The desktop icons were completely different. In her scattered rush to leave, she had taken Keith's laptop by mistake. She called him and he was on his way over. While talking she noticed an icon entitled OCC. She clicked and opened it. It showed everything there was to know about her company, including detailed information on nearly everyone there.

She really didn't mean to be nosy. She was just curious. Truth was, she had a file on him, as well, although hers wasn't nearly as complete. She had no idea who did his research, but they were very thorough. She opened Bill's personnel file.

It showed everything, including exactly what he was doing involving payoffs and bribes for Lester Jameson. It even showed that the woman from Los Angeles who stood up at the Community Center was actually Lester Jameson's mistress, paid by Bill to be there. Then she saw a notation entitled Probability Factor. It noted two words—will betray. Gia nodded, realizing Keith knew all along what was going on and she didn't have a clue. When he had told her at one point to consider herself warned, she should have listened.

Then she opened the file entitled Gianna Duncan. She read slowly, seeing her entire life written down, including every man she'd ever dated. "Where in the world did he get all this?" she muttered. Family, friends, they were all listed. Then she saw her probability factors. It noted that getting close to her and forming an emotional bond would guarantee a favorable endorsement from OCC and could tip the electoral scales in his father's favor.

She knew exactly what she was looking at. This was a game plan on how to manipulate her to get what he wanted. It occurred to her that all this time with Keith was just a cleverly thought out rouse to get an endorsement for his father.

It was just as Bill "the betrayer" had told her. She just wouldn't listen. She'd been played from the very beginning. But he had warned her not to underestimate him. She couldn't believe it. He lied about everything, including his feelings for her, just to get an endorsement. "He lied," she said out loud.

"Gia," Keith said, standing in the office doorway. It was obvious he'd been there awhile. He had to know what she was reading.

"You told me and I didn't listen."

"Gia…"

She shook her head. "You even warned me that you were going to do this to me," she said firmly.

"Gia, that was a long time before."

"Before what, you got what you wanted from me? The election is Tuesday. You have my blessing. Go. It's over."

"It's not over. I love you, Gia," he said softly.

She laughed. "Oh, wait, what is this, another game, another manipulation? What do you want from me now? What's left?"

"Yes, it started out with me wanting the endorsement, but that's not how it is now. I swear to that. I love you. Please..."

"Please what?" She closed the laptop gently and picked it up and tossed it to him. He caught it as she knew he would. "Get out. You got what you came for."

Bonnie came to the office door and looked at Gia's and Keith's faces. "I guess you just heard that you're all over the news."

"Who?" Gia asked.

"Both of you," she said. "Bill said that Keith bought your endorsement and he has proof. Danny has pictures on his blog of you two kissing at somebody's house last night. Then he has more of you at dinner and then you kissing at the same house this morning. What do you want me to do, a press release?"

Gia shook her head and turned away. "Bonnie, give us a minute," Keith said. Bonnie nodded and left.

"My credibility is ruined. I have nothing."

"Gia, I didn't mean to—"

"Of course you did. You just didn't mean to get caught."

"Gia, listen to me."

"It really is all about money, power and ego, isn't it? For you, my father, my grandfather. You always have to win no matter who gets hurt in the end. Your team has to beat the other team. What about the people in the middle who suffer? Yeah, you're just like my grandfather and my father. All you ever care about is getting what you want. You don't care who you hurt. You don't care about me. You never did."

"Gia, you don't understand. This will help you, trust me."

"On the contrary, Keith, I understand completely," she said. "You did what you did. It's done. You ruined OCC's reputation and my credibility just to get your father reelected. Congratulations, you won. Goodbye."

He didn't respond. He nodded, turned and left. She watched him go, then stared at the empty doorway realizing this was it; it was over. She walked over to her desk and sat down, then looked up when she heard a soft knock. Her father was standing in the doorway. He walked in, going straight to the Chinese puzzle box, then opened it.

"I thought you didn't remember how to open that," she said.

He smiled. "I guess I remember when I need to." He looked at her and half smiled. "Are you okay?"

"No, I'm not okay."

He nodded and glanced back at the door. "I heard."

She nodded tearfully, shrugged and looked around the room. "I guess this is over. So much for my family legacy."

"This isn't your family legacy, Gia. This is—"

"Dad, not now. This isn't the time to extol the

virtues of foreclosures, bait and switch and cheating people out of their homes just to take their property and get richer."

"That's not what I do and not why I'm here. I know I haven't been much of a father or a friend. I lost sight of all that a long time ago. But I need you to hear me now. This, all this is important, but it's nothing compared to what you just gave up."

"What did I give up?"

"Do you love him?"

She took a deep breath. "He used me. He got what he wanted."

"Yes, probably, but I have a feeling that his betrayal ended a while ago. That man left here with love in his eyes. Believe me, it's a hard world out there when you don't have the one you love at your side." She didn't reply. He nodded and turned back to the open door. "And by the way, Duncan Real Estate Development has changed a lot since you walked away. We tried to change you, but you changed me instead. Stop by. I think you'd like what you see."

She tried not to smile, but she did.

Keith walked out, where he saw Bonnie at her desk. She looked up at him. "Um, I'm sorry. I heard. But if you want my two cents, I think you two make the perfect couple."

"Yeah, me, too," Keith said.

"I saw the picture Danny posted of you in the Diamond District coming out of the store," she said, smiling. "Did you get it?" He nodded. She smiled. "Good."

Keith glanced back toward Gia's office. "I hope so."

"Um, about what Bill said, questioning Gia's reputation. What can she do about it, a press release or something?"

Keith shook his head. "No, I got this."

The rest of the weekend was a rush of publicity, but Bill's mediocre attempts at hogging the limelight were nothing compared to Keith's consummate charm. When Keith vowed to Bonnie that he had this, sure enough, he did. As soon as he left the OCC office Saturday afternoon, he called Megan. He detailed his process and she put it into motion. By the eleven o'clock news, Bill's comment and accusations had turned into a pathetic attempt to justify his existence. He ended his fifteen minutes of fame by promising to run for mayor in four years. No one took him seriously.

OCC's reputation was intact and Gia's credibility as a community organizer had never been stronger. She held her regular Monday night neighborhood meeting, and although there were a good number of additional faces, the crowd was totally interested in what she spoke about. At first she had no idea what to expect when she walked into the meeting hall. But she soon realized that everyone there was interested in a better life and her apparent close affiliation with

Keith Washington gave her additional influence with the city's mayor.

Apparently she was wrong.

For the last two and a half days she had watched Keith work his magic from the safety of her home and office. She wanted him with all her heart, and she knew it wasn't pride that kept her from going to him, it was trust. She loved him and in her heart she knew he loved her, too. But how could she trust him?

Chapter 22

On Election Day Keith's focus was back on Blake. But even with that it was obvious that he was merely going through the motions. Still, it kept him busy and distracted from what was really eating him apart inside. He had Megan and Kate out in the field taking care of any last-minute glitches. Prudence and Michael were at the Grand Hotel preparing for the party of the decade. His brothers were roaming the voting sites shaking hands and meeting voters.

He stayed, managing it all from his office. Thankfully he was alone, having given everyone the day off. He watched the exit polls and communicated nonstop with his mother and father, both making late public appearances. With the exception of a few last-minute crises, everything was under control.

"All right, that's it. Enough's enough. You need to deal with this thing now."

Keith looked up from his computer to see his brothers walk into his office. He sighed heavily and leaned back in the chair, knowing this was going to be more nonsense that he had to deal with. "What is it?" he asked anxiously.

"Bro, you're killing us. You need to go get her and stop driving everyone crazy," Drew said.

"What?" Keith repeated.

"You know what, Gia Duncan. You need to tell her you love her and give her that ring burning a hole in your pocket."

Keith looked at his brothers. There was no denying it. They were crazy and today of all days he didn't need to hear this. But they knew him too well. "I wish I could. But she won't have me."

"So what do you do, mope around here the rest of your life?"

"You know you're overlooking the obvious. You can always talk to the expert," Drew said.

"Who's the expert?" Keith asked. Then he knew and shook his head. Drew nodded and looked at Jeremy, nodding, too.

"Mamma Lou," they said.

"No," Keith insisted.

"Actually, you don't have much of a choice."

"What did you do?" Keith asked.

They smiled and turned to leave. Drew opened the door. "Come on in, Mamma Lou. We're through with him."

Keith glared at his brothers as Louise walked into his office and they left smiling happily.

"Mamma Lou, I know what you're gonna say and I appreciate your interest, but this is—"

"Love," she interrupted, smiling. "Yes, I know."

"No, this is not a good time. I have to—"

"Although I'm not quite sure how you two got it all tangled up like this."

Keith knew there was no use. She wasn't listening to him. "I know you wanted Gia with Rick and I know..."

"Rick Renault is a sweetheart, yes. And matching him up will be my pleasure, but honey, he and Gia could never be a match."

"But at the Ball. You—"

"He was just a nice young man who helped me out with a little push in the right direction."

Keith understood. He nodded. "It was me all along."

"Oh, don't say it like that. You and Gia are perfect together. You have fire together, and the spark you two ignite is a joy to watch. That's love."

"That was love. I messed up."

"Of course you didn't. All will turn out exactly as it's supposed to. Love has a way of making sure of that."

"Are you sure about that?" he said.

"Oh, yes, love is forever and you, my dear, have a forever love."

"I like that, a forever love."

"Now come on. I have a celebration to attend and a little errand to run first."

Gia watched Tuesday night. Three hours after the polls closed, the votes had been counted and the official announcement was made. There were gatherings and parties all over the city. But the main celebration was at the Grand Hotel Ballroom, and it seemed as if the entire city showed up.

Although invited, she didn't feel like going out. She didn't have a whole lot to celebrate. Yes, she had endorsed Blake Washington and yes, he won the election, but what she lost was far more. Her cell phone rang. It was her grandmother.

"Hi, Grandmom, how are you doing?"

"Fine, I'm having the time of my life."

"Doing what?" Gia asked. She had no idea how anyone could have the time of their life at a nursing home.

"Celebrating."

"Oh, right, the election. I didn't know the Crestar was doing anything."

"Oh, I'm not at Crestar. I took the night off."

"What? Where are you?"

"Louise invited me. I'm at the Grand Hotel."

"Grandmom, what?"

Julia chuckled. "You should come down and join us. We're in the Washington Suite."

"I'll be right there." Gia didn't think and she didn't waste any time. She changed and hurried to the hotel. The crowd was insane. There was no way she was getting in. She called her grandmother and told her. A few minutes later she was instructed to go to the employee entrance. Megan, Keith's assistant, stood waiting and escorted her to the suite.

She hugged and kissed her grandmother and Louise and watched the large television as several speakers began the program. She saw Keith standing on the stage along with his brothers and sister. Then she saw what he had in his hand. It was perfect. She texted him. Now.

She watched as a few seconds later he looked at his cell phone. His expression was priceless. Her heart soared. He texted her back.

Keith: Where?

Gia: Here. Washington Suite.

She watched as he stared at the small screen, waiting, smiled and then texted something and finally walked away. She stood. Her heart raced. This was it.

Keith ran so fast he doubted his feet even touched the floor. He knew the elevator would be too slow, so he dashed up seven floors. A minute later he opened the door to see Mamma Lou and Julia Duncan smiling and pointing to the next room. He rushed in. Gia was standing there, smiling. He was speechless.

"So, I was thinking, maybe waking up with you every morning and hanging out with you wouldn't be too bad."

He smiled and nodded, remembering the conversation. "I agree. Come on. We need to get downstairs. I need to be onstage and you need to be with me," he said. She nodded and they left.

Minutes later Gia was on the stage with the rest of the Washington family. She got warm welcoming hugs from everyone as the program began. Preston Hodge, who had also won a seat on the city council, stepped up to the podium to introduce Marian Washington.

Blake stepped up and stood beside Keith.

"Congratulations, son," Blake said, shaking Keith's hand.

"I think you have that backward, Dad. Congratulations to you. You're mayor of Philadelphia again. There was never any doubt you'd be here."

Blake nodded. "Are you ready for this?"

Keith nodded. "Yes, I'm ready."

"I don't often get in my sons' personal lives, but when it affects more than his life I don't have a choice. Your happiness affects all of us. Loyalty to family is admirable, but loyalty to love is without a doubt life's true joy. Gia is a wonderful woman and I'm proud of you."

Keith smiled and nodded. "Thanks, Dad."

Marian Washington stepped up on the stage and stood at the podium. The crowd of thousands was still loud and celebrating. She held her hands up and after a few minutes they finally settled down. "Thank you, Preston, thank you and congratulations." The crowd roared again. "This is an incredible night," she continued. The cheers began again. "I want to thank you all so much for staying and for coming out tonight. And a special thanks to all you volunteers. It's a great night. What do you think?"

The crowd went wild again. Marian smiled and waved, then laughed as a chant of "Wash-ing-ton" began. "Okay, okay," she said, calming them down again, "my job tonight is to introduce my husband. I'm not going to tell you all the wonderful things about him because you already know that. And I'm not going to tell everything he's done for this city because you already know that, too. I am going to tell you that he's the best man I know and the man of my heart. Ladies and gentlemen, my husband, your newly reelected mayor, Blake Washington."

The noise level was earsplitting as she barely got the words out. The music started playing and balloons fell from the ceiling. Blake stepped up to the podium, and the party began all over again. He kissed his wife and they waved.

After another three minutes of constant cheering, Blake stepped up to begin his acceptance speech. "Thank you, Philadelphia," he began. "Okay, before I get started I got a text message request a few minutes ago. So I'm gonna yield this moment to a very special couple in my life. Son?" He turned to Keith.

Keith nodded, took Gia's hand and stepped away from the crowed stage. He knelt down and Gia gasped. She looked into his eyes, knowing the moment was here. Tears rolled down her face. The crowd immediately hushed to complete silence. "Gia, I love you and I need to love you for the rest of my life. This is forever. We are a forever love. Please honor me and become my wife."

Her hands shook, her legs weakened and her

voice escaped her. But the tears rolled steadily as she smiled and nodded, barely speaking the one word. "Yes."

The ballroom erupted.

"Now, that's what I call a celebration," Julia said, witnessing the proposal on television with her dear friend beside her.

Louise nodded. "Indeed. That's what I call a forever love."

* * * * *

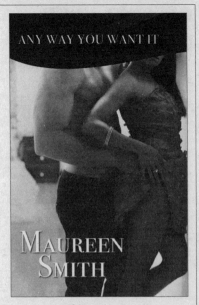

REQUEST YOUR FREE BOOKS!

2 FREE NOVELS
PLUS 2 FREE GIFTS!

KIMANI™
ROMANCE

Love's ultimate destination!

KROM11B

He's her everything—she just doesn't know it yet!

Essence **bestselling author**

DONNA HILL

KIMANI ROMANCE

EVERYTHING IS *You*

LAWSONS *of* LOUISIANA

DONNA HILL

ESSENCE BESTSELLING AUTHOR

EVERYTHING IS *You*

When Jacqueline Lawson returns home to Baton Rouge, she's hiding a secret—one she's determined to keep. But Raymond Jordan has sworn to uncover all her secrets, and her on-again, off-again lover will not let her get away once more. The passion's as hot as ever between them, but love means putting yourself in the line of fire. Is Jacqueline ready to risk her heart?

LAWSONS *of* LOUISIANA

"Delightful."
—*RT Book Reviews* on *HEART'S REWARD*

HARLEQUIN®
www.Harlequin.com

*Available December 2012
wherever books are sold!*

KPDH2841212

Will love be waiting at the finish line?

RACING HEARTS

MICHELLE MONKOU

KIMANI ROMANCE

MICHELLE MONKOU

Dedicated doctor Erin Wilson lives her life cautiously—the opposite of Marc Newton, world-famous race-car driver and her newest patient. But Erin is determined to keep him off the track so he can heal from an injury. Resisting the seductive millionaire playboy's advances takes sheer grit, because Marc is set on racing again…and winning her heart!

"An engaging love story."
—*RT Book Reviews* on *SWEET SURRENDER*

HARLEQUIN®
™ www.Harlequin.com

*Available December 2012
wherever books are sold!*

KPMM2871212

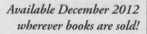